WHERE THE DARKNESS ENDS

ALICIA RADES

CHAPTER 1

When my eyes opened, I could tell it was cold outside. The snow was gently falling past my window and piling at the bottom of the sill, displaying the beautiful—yet typical—Christmas scene. Despite the obvious chilly weather, it was bright, gently illuminating the room and creating a blissful ambiance.

I stretched my arms above my head, pulled my legs in the opposite direction, and took in a deep, refreshing yawn. As I did so, I rolled to the opposite side of the bed, ending right on top of Adam.

"Hmm..." he moaned in a somewhat suggestive manner. "Good morning, beautiful."

"Good morning to you, too, love of my life," I replied.

Adam wrapped his arms around me and pulled me in, planting a kiss on my lips that made the butterflies in my stomach spring to life. Although we'd already been engaged for six months and been together nearly four years, I still got excited each time we touched. I hoped that feeling would never go away.

I pulled away from him and stared into his eyes. He gave a half smile before speaking. "What?"

"Nothing," I told him. "I just love to look at you."

I really did love to look at him. His gorgeous smile is what made me notice him in the first place back when we were both studying nursing. It was my first year, so I didn't know anyone at school; I'd only lived in Illinois for a year and hadn't made very many friends.

"Do you remember when we met?" I asked. "I was hiding out in the library, and I remember sitting at one of the round study tables by myself when I heard your voice. I looked up from my book to see you chatting with the librarian."

"I'll never forget it," he said with a smile.

I closed my eyes and took in the memory.

I watched his beautiful eyes scan the room. Our eyes met for a brief instant before I buried myself back in my book. I lifted it slightly so he couldn't see I was blushing.

He was so gorgeous. There was something about his smile that made my heart flutter. His smile stretched across his face and showed off his straight white teeth and a line of gums below his upper lip. When he smiled, a line of wrinkles formed near the corner of his eyes.

His eyes were stunning, too. I knew without studying them that I could easily lose myself in their grey-blue brilliance.

He turned, and I ducked behind my book again. I didn't hear him approach until he spoke. "You're taking Moore's class?"

I looked up at him. "Huh?"

"Your textbook," he said, pointing to the book in my hands. "That class is taught by Caroline Moore, isn't it?"

Without letting me answer, he continued, telling me about how much he enjoyed her class before eventually moving on to more personal subjects.

"I'm Adam, by the way," he said, extending his hand.

I was still holding my book up to my face, trying to mask the red flame that was surely rising from my pale white cheeks.

Few guys had ever talked to me. Most people saw me behind my books and figured I didn't want to be disturbed. Most of the time, I didn't.

I wasn't good with words, at least the ones that came out of my mouth. I was always tripping over my tongue and never knew what to say. Despite my anxiety, his friendly gesture calmed me down, and something about the entire situation felt familiar and comfortable, like sugar-coated déjà vu.

I lowered my book, face still crimson, and took ahold of his *hand. As we touched, a spark jumped between our fingers. It was that kind of spark you read about in books yet never believe until it happens to you. It took me by surprise.*

My face flamed more vigorously, and my heart raced faster.

"Liz," I croaked. I cleared my throat. "Liz," I tried again, this time with a bit more confidence.

Adam went on to ask questions about my major and where I was from. As we spoke, the nerves tangling in my belly gently faded, and I quickly became comfortable in his company. By the end of the conversation, he had asked me out for that Friday night. Through some miracle, I was able to move my lips and agree to the invite.

As nervous as I was, the experience was magical. We both instantly felt a connection, later admitting to each other that it felt like we'd met before.

"In a past life," Adam would joke.

After our first date, we were practically inseparable. I was surprised at how comfortable I felt around him. I'd never been much for socializing, let alone with a man. His gaze, his touch, and his smile all quickly brought the butterflies in my stomach to life, but at the same time, it soothed me. Our love was equally passionate as it was peaceful.

Bringing myself back into the present, I continued looking into his eyes, falling in love with his smile for another countless time and taking note of every aspect of his beautiful features—the dark blonde hair that fell near his bright blue eyes, still unkempt from the night; the small dimple he got on the right side of his face when he smiled; and the few freckles scattered along the bridge of his nose.

He grabbed hold of me and rolled us both over to the opposite side of the bed. With him now on top of me, I wrapped my legs around his waist and pulled him close. He kissed my forehead, then my nose, and finally my lips before moving to my neck, down to my collar bone, and then even further down my body. The way his lips felt against my skin gave me a sensation that went deeper than the butterflies in my stomach.

His lips came back up to meet mine before he propped himself above me and looked down at me. His right hand moved from the bed to my forehead as he brushed my blonde hair from my face. His dreamy eyes stared into mine. He smiled and mouthed, *I love you.*

"I love you, too," I whispered back.

"How are you feeling?" he asked.

He was always checking up on me, and I loved how much he cared. So often, I woke up feeling fatigued or with a headache, but my symptoms had been under control for a while now.

"It's a good day," I told him.

He took his eyes off me and glanced toward the clock.

"Jesus," he cried as he jumped out of bed. "It's already eight-thirty! We're supposed to be at my parents' at ten, and it takes over an hour to get there."

I propped myself up on my elbow and watched him frantically race around the room, silently giggling at him. He picked up clothes and tossed them aside until he found his towel in the mess.

He stood there naked, looked at me, and asked, "Are you going to join?"

"Sure," I agreed as I pulled the covers off and climbed out of bed. "But I don't understand what the hurry is. There's no reason that we have to be at your parents' house *exactly* at ten o'clock."

"It's a little thing called *tradition*," he replied.

I suppose I didn't really understand. I didn't care much for Christmas, and tradition meant little in my family. After my mom died when I was twelve, we stopped going to church, and my dad and I didn't do much for Christmas except exchange gifts.

Adam's family loved Christmas and threw a huge party every year. Each Christmas Eve, we arrived at Jim and Sue's at ten, where we visited and helped with Christmas dinner until one o'clock. That's when everyone sat down for a feast, and then we all exchanged gifts *one at a time*, until we ended the night with Christmas Eve service at their local church at five.

Adam and I quickly took our shower and got dressed. Heaven forbid I should wear jeans to a family gathering. I slipped on my sleek black evening dress that fell to my knees and added a simple heart-shaped necklace and a fancy set of sandals. I tried piling my hair atop my head, but with my stick-straight locks, I just couldn't manage it. In the end, I simply let my hair fall to my shoulders.

Adam put on a pair of fancy black pants paired with a white collared shirt and a Christmas-themed tie with snowmen and snowflakes on it.

I felt like the fancy dress was somewhat going overboard, but if I was going to be part of his family, I had to put up with these ridiculous traditions.

It wasn't like I didn't like his family. I did. I just wasn't too fond of a Christmas party that included a family tree of four generations.

Adam and I loaded up the car and drove away from our two-bedroom duplex. We lived north-west of Chicago in what I considered a small town. The city limits sign read ten thousand people, but since we could get to the city within an hour without passing farmland, Adam argued that this was by no means a *small town*. He claimed any landlord in a small town would let us have a dog. I promised him we'd get a dog once we bought our own place.

It didn't take long to hit farmland as we headed west. Adam's parents lived an hour away in the middle of nowhere. I would hardly call it a town. Their home was located on about five acres, and it overlooked a small lake.

Adam drove as I looked out the window and watched the dull scenery pass by. Snow gently blanketed the earth, but the sky was a hazy gray. The world was flat as the eye could see. It was times like this when I longed for the snow-capped mountains of the Salt Lake Valley, but I knew if I went back home, I would only dream of the fresh smell of spring, bright greens of summer, and dazzling change of leaves in autumn.

It occurred to me that I probably wouldn't get a chance to talk with my father the rest of the day, and I wanted to wish him a Merry Christmas. Even though we'd stopped going to church ages ago, I knew he'd appreciate it.

I loved talking to my dad. He'd always been my best friend.

I pulled my cell phone from my bag. When he picked up, there was a hint of laughter in his voice, as if someone had just told him a great joke. Surely Janelle was there, and he was probably laughing at something she'd said.

My father had been dating Janelle for over a year. After I left home—which my dad begged me not to do even though I needed a fresh start—he finally decided it would be okay to start dating again. I didn't mind. I knew he needed someone to keep him company. Out of all the girls he'd gone through over the past five years, I think I liked Janelle the best.

Janelle was fond of my father, and I could tell by the joy in his voice that he was happy with her, too. Plus, she was nice. She'd already sent me a Christmas present for this year, and when I opened the package, my jaw dropped. It was a brand-new eReader. She'd remembered how much I enjoyed reading from our previous conversations.

"Hello," my father greeted.

"Hi, Dad."

"Hey, sweetie, how's your Christmas Eve going?" He let out another giggle. He was obviously having a great Christmas Eve of his own.

"Not much has happened so far," I informed him. "We're headed to Adam's parents'. We're on the road."

The dogs barked in the background, and I could hear his cockatoos squawking. Dad was a zoologist and loved animals. My father and I continued with the small talk for a while, until he asked what we were having for dinner.

"I'm sure Sue will make a feast," I told him with a chuckle.

"I'm trying your mother's honey glazed ham recipe," he said proudly. "It smells really good. I wish you were here to share it with."

My stomach twisted at the mention of my mother. "I wish I were there, too, Dad."

"Your mother loved Christmas," he said. "She used to hang lights all throughout the house. It took her hours."

"I remember." I tried to keep my voice steady.

"I dug the angel tree topper out of storage," he continued. "I thought I might try to get back into the Christmas spirit."

"That's great, Dad. Um… We're almost there," I lied. "I'm going to have to let you go."

"Okay, love you, sweetie."

"Love you, too, Dad. Bye."

Silence filled the car, and Adam reached over to squeeze my hand. He didn't say anything, and he didn't need to.

My father seemed like a completely different person since he started dating again. He seemed younger and more energetic. I'm sure he'd tell me the same thing. He'd remarked about how different I'd become since I met Adam. He told me I was more social and seemed happier.

"I found a cool rock the other day." Adam's voice cut through the silence, and he reached into the cup holder to pull out a shiny red rock. He was trying to distract me, and it was working.

I flipped the rock over in my hands, inspecting the intricate lines running through it. "This is neat. Where'd you find it?"

"In the parking lot when I was leaving work," he said. "What do you think? Does it deserve a place in my collection?"

I smiled and handed it back to him. "Definitely."

Adam must've noticed I didn't want to talk, because he turned on our favorite radio station. He sang along to the music, and I listened to the soothing sound of his voice.

I spent the rest of the ride silently wishing to be back in Salt Lake, where I could marvel at the mountains and spend time with my dad instead of visiting with people I hardly knew. But this mattered to Adam. Instead, I took a few deep breaths and prepared myself for what I knew would be an uncomfortable situation.

CHAPTER 2

It took longer than expected to reach Adam's parents' house because of the weather. The snowfall started out soft, but if the forecast was any prediction, it looked like we were going to get dumped on today.

"The perfect white Christmas," Adam said brightly as he pulled into his parents' driveway.

It was almost eleven by the time we arrived.

Adam hurried to the trunk to grab the presents. "Looks like we're the last ones here."

I stepped out of the car and slipped on the icy drive-way, but I caught myself on the open door. After I straightened myself up, I reached into the back of the car, grabbed the cookies and presents that I'd brought along, and walked with Adam and his full arms to the door.

His parents' house was huge, tucked behind the trees on a dead-end road with a large private yard to go along with it. His father was a physician, so they grew up with quite a bit of money. The exterior of the house displayed a log-cabin style, but the inside was elaborately decorated with family pictures and tacky décor that said things like *Home is Where the Heart Is*.

We entered, and even with its vast foyer that opened to a second level balcony, the home still seemed crowded. People from every room seemed to perk up like a dog that just spotted a squirrel when we walked in.

"They're here!" his mom, Sue, screamed from the kitchen.

His uncle piped up from the living room, "Look who decided to make an appearance."

His nephew came running from one of the first-story bedrooms screaming, "Uncle Adam!"

It seemed everyone decided to crowd us, taking turns saying hello and exchanging hugs, even though I hadn't had time to put down the boxes in my hands.

Sue dried her hands on a towel, then pushed her auburn curls out of her eyes. She took her apron off and walked towards us, arms open.

"Adam," she sang as she kissed him on the cheek. "Elizabeth." Sue put her hands on mine, which were still holding gifts, and kissed my cheek.

"Liz," I corrected her.

She looked down as if she suddenly noticed the pile in my hands. "Here, let me take that."

Adam led me to the living room. "Liz, you remember my uncle David. And my aunt Sherry, my sister Stacy, my brother Brian. And Chris, you know Liz, and oh, my grandma Doris."

This went on for a while until Adam finished naming the thirty or so people in the house, from his grandparents to his aunts and uncles, four siblings, and nieces and nephews. I smiled and shook hands, but I didn't remember most of their names. I mostly just stood there with a smile on my face, trying to mask how uncomfortable I was.

After initial introductions, we found a place to sit along the ledge of the fireplace, which illuminated fake flames.

It wasn't even two seconds before Adam's aunt Sherry asked, "So, when are you two kids getting hitched again?"

"We're twenty-three," Adam informed her. "I hardly think that qualifies us as kids."

"Okay, okay." She let out a horrendous giggle and threw her head back, which shook the drink in her hand —yes, she was already drinking—and corrected herself. "When are you two *adults* getting married?"

Adam smiled. "February first."

People went on to ask us about what we were doing with our lives, where we were working, and when we were going to have kids. We quickly dodged that last question, giving a non-answer. This continued until the conversation shifted to Sherry's latest topic of her book club.

I took this opportunity to escape the crowd and headed for the kitchen, where Sue was preparing lunch.

"Need help?" I asked.

She looked up from the dish she was preparing. "Of course, Elizabeth. Here." She handed me a bowl and pointed to the pile of veggies sitting on the counter. "Cut those up and make it pretty."

We stood in silence for what seemed like several minutes, tending to our own tasks, until she took it upon herself to break the silence. "So, Elizabeth, when you and Adam get married, can I expect another grandchild within nine months?"

I gave a half-hearted smile. "I don't know about that. You might have to wait a while."

What I really meant was, *You're never getting grandchildren.* I didn't know how to tell her that. It'd break her heart.

"Don't make me wait too long," she teased. "I expect kids out of each and every one of my children."

She was trying to make light of the comment, but she might as well have shoved her knife through my gut. I finished cutting the veggies and wiped down the counter before rushing out of there as fast as I could so she couldn't continue harping on me about giving her grandchildren.

The harassment didn't get any better in the next room. I thought I'd be safe in the room the kids were playing in, but it wasn't long until one of Adam's nieces asked if I was going to have a baby like her mom was. Lila was one of the few kids whose names I remembered. She was named after Adam's deceased grandmother and apparently reminded everyone of her.

"Not right now," I told Lila with a nervous chuckle. I ducked out of the room as fast as I could. In the hall, I bumped into his grandma, who was returning to the living room from the bathroom.

"I'm sorry, dear," she apologized. Her eyes drifted into the room the kids were playing in. "I love my great grandkids to death, but those kids can be wild. It's different when they're your own," she assured me, patting my shoulder. "Don't worry, I'm sure you're not far off from that."

That's when I started to break down. I couldn't stand everyone asking me when I was going to have kids. I felt the tears welling up inside me, and my chest compressed until I felt I was going to break. I could feel the tension building inside my body as I tried to hold in the tears.

"Yeah, I'm sure. Please excuse me," I said in a choked attempt to mask my emotions. I quickly moved past her and headed for the bathroom.

Once I locked myself inside, I let my emotions run free as the tears streamed down my face. It wasn't that I didn't want children. In fact, I would love to have children. But I couldn't have them, and it hurt unlike anything else.

I always dreamed of being a mother, but when I was a teen, I was diagnosed with endometriosis. The illness caused tissue from my uterus to grow on other parts of my body, which damaged my reproductive organs and messed with my hormones—ultimately leaving me infertile. Adam knew, but it felt wrong to tell his family, especially at Christmas. I didn't want people feeling sorry for me, and it was best right now to simply let them enjoy their Christmas.

I sat on the lip of the tub, rubbing my eyes with a tissue and trying to ease the knot in my stomach. I didn't feel sorry for myself, but I felt a rush of emotions —anger, sorrow, disappointment—knowing that I could never be a mother and that there was nothing I could do about it. Today was just a sore reminder.

I finally managed to calm myself down, and I

decided to face the crowd again. I took a few deep breaths and attempted to relax my face to bring my color back to normal. I dug through a few drawers before I found some makeup, and I wiped a bit of mascara on my face to make it seem like I wasn't in here crying. I took another deep breath and headed back to the party.

I sat silently and listened to conversation and watched TV with the rest of the family, not saying a word until Sue finally called everyone for lunch. People gathered around the dining room table while others sat around fold-up tables and the children found their seats on even smaller tables.

Sherry offered me a drink, but I refused. She poured me a glass anyway, but I didn't drink it. Alcohol would only trigger my symptoms. People thought endometriosis was all about abdominal pain and bad cramping, but when things got bad, that pain permeated my entire body. Not to mention the chronic fatigue, migraines, and nausea that had led to me passing out more than once. A glass of wine was usually fine, but I was careful with my diet to minimize my risk of a flare-up.

After stuffing ourselves with potatoes, gravy, ham, and other delicious holiday entrées, everything seemed to quiet down as people gathered in the living room for the gift exchange. This literally went on for hours because in Adam's family tradition, you had to see exactly what everyone else got and watch each person open their present. Luckily, they were the type of people who ripped the paper quickly instead of trying to save the wrapping.

I watched as family members tore open their gifts and jumped up and down when they got what they wanted, and I graciously smiled each time someone thanked me for the gifts I gave them. I offered the same thanks back when it was my turn to open presents.

By the time we were all swimming in wrapping paper, it was almost five o'clock, which meant it was time to head to the church service. Not everyone decided to go, and even though Adam didn't go to church year-round, he believed the Christmas service was important, so for the sake of tradition, I tagged along. We each hopped in our separate vehicles and headed down the road to the church, past the thick rows of trees and other elaborate homes.

I wasn't really one for going to church. I'd explored the idea of God, and it just didn't make sense to me.

I sat in silence, listening to the sermon but not taking it to heart. Children worked their way to the front and told the story of the birth of Jesus, and we sang Christmas songs. I stood up each time we had to sing, but I never actually opened my mouth.

It was strange participating in these traditions I didn't believe in. I was positive that when you died, there was nothing but nonexistence and darkness. Did I hope there was an afterlife? Of course I did. I wanted there to be a hint of light where the darkness ends, but I wasn't expecting it.

The service ended, and Adam and I made our way back to our car. By now, the weather had progressed worse than the forecast had predicted. It was practically blizzarding, coating the road in an icy sheet, and the bitter cold nipped at my cheeks. Adam took my hand, and I pulled my hood over my head. We ran as fast as we could without slipping until we reached the car.

Once we ducked into the vehicle, Adam turned to me. "That wasn't awful, was it?"

"No," I insisted. "It was a lovely service. Just because I don't agree with your beliefs doesn't mean the service wasn't beautiful."

"Thanks, that means a lot." He leaned over and kissed me lightly on the lips. "I appreciate your support. Let's get out of this cold."

He started the car, and we headed out of the parking

lot and onto the slick, icy road, fishtailing a bit as we turned. The car slowly crept down a steep hill.

"Wow, these roads are really bad," I remarked.

"Yeah," Adam agreed. "But we're not that far from home. We'll make it."

He gripped my hand to assure me of this and gazed at me with dreamy eyes. Then he moved his eyes back toward the road and placed both hands on the wheel.

That's when it happened. Neither of us saw it coming, and who could? In this weather, we could hardly see anything. It snuck up on us in an instant. My heart jumped into my throat, and I gripped my seat tightly, bracing myself. Everything began moving in slow motion.

The headlights moved from the road, to the trees, then back toward the church, continuing around and around. Adam's eyes widened, his face struck with horror. He tried desperately to control the car, but didn't succeed. I heard a high-pitched scream in my ear, not realizing it was my own. A rush of terror rose inside me, making me freeze, yet pumping my heart at an incredible rate.

And then I watched as a tree moved closer and closer to the car until suddenly, I became a part of it, wrapped around the tree, smashed as easily as if someone stepped on a soda can. Just like the car crumpled, so did my skull.

One second I was watching Adam's glorious, smiling face, promising to keep me safe, and the next instant I saw nothing.

I was broken and bleeding, and I was no longer breathing.

CHAPTER 3

For what seemed like just a brief moment, everything went dark. I saw the world spinning around us, the car acting as a pivot point. I heard my scream of terror, and I felt excruciating pain running from my head out toward the rest of my body.

That was it.

The entire thing lasted only a split second, and then as quick as the pain came, it was gone.

I woke up aware that I was still alive. I couldn't sense my surroundings, as if every sensor in my body had shut down. I couldn't taste the air, see where I was, or feel anything. The only indication I was still alive was the thoughts racing through my head.

Perhaps I'm not awake at all, I thought. *I must be sleeping, or possibly seriously injured and under anesthetics.*

I was aware that I sustained very serious injuries, but I wasn't quite sure how much time had passed since the accident. To me, it seemed like only seconds ago, but there was no longer any pain.

I tried playing it back in my head, but all I could see was a flash of spinning headlights and a quick, almost unrecognizable image of a tree as the brightness of the headlights intensified in my retinas. Each time I replayed the crash, I knew it ended in pain. If this only happened seconds ago, why was I no longer feeling this pain? Did the crash leave me paralyzed?

I wasn't sure of anything at that moment. Everything seemed so disorienting, unlike anything I'd ever experienced. It was like all I had left of me was my mind—like my body was no longer connected to my thoughts.

I was seconds away from accepting that I'd passed out when I heard a voice call out to me. A faint, distant voice. No. Not a voice.

What . . . what was that? It wasn't me. I was sure of that. Someone was calling out to me, but I still couldn't hear. How did I know they were calling out to me?

There were no words. Wherever I was, I couldn't sense spoken language, but someone was trying to communicate with me. I struggled to reach back to them and let them know I was still alive.

I felt a presence next to me. It was like knowing

someone is watching you when you couldn't hear or see them. I pushed myself a little bit harder to understand this concept and to connect with the being near me. As I reached out, I got the feeling that the person was trying to say, "Welcome home."

It was as if someone said those words directly to me, but I couldn't get in touch with my senses and actually *hear* the words.

"Are you okay?" The voice seemed to show serious concern for my condition. But that was it. Concern. I never heard a voice. I never heard words. But someone next to me was somehow communicating their concern for my well-being, and I understood each thought of theirs.

I tried to speak back, but I couldn't find my lips or my tongue to formulate the words I needed.

The being continued to show worry for me, but it became more alarmed as I tried to find my body within all the confusion. I became aware of more people surrounding me, each conveying their own emotions onto me.

Everything seemed so confusing and muddled as I tried to make sense of what was going on. There were now at least three distinct beings surrounding me, creating their own thoughts and communicating them between each other.

"She'll be alright," one person said—or rather thought.

"I've seen it before," another told them at the same time.

"I don't understand," the first one—I think—told the other two.

"It's rare, but it happens," the second one replied.

They continued arguing about something, but with so many thoughts overlapping each other, it was difficult to focus on what was actually going on. I tried to quiet them down. I looked for my lips again, but I couldn't find them. Giving up on my search and becoming frustrated, I threw my emotions at each one of them.

Quiet! I tried to say.

As if they all heard me, the conversations instantly stopped. It was silent in my head again, but I could still feel their presence. Now that I had their attention, I slowly tried to formulate the thought I'd been thinking since they appeared, and I threw it at all three of them.

"Who are you, and what are you doing in my head?" I asked.

As if they understood how emotionally frustrated and confused I was, they took turns with their thoughts this time.

"Can we all please calm down?" a woman, it felt like,

said. "It's hard enough to communicate when there aren't high emotions racing around."

As if to calm me, another one took a turn. "Let's start with introductions. Hi, I'm Eric."

"And I'm Anna," the woman said.

"Darryl," the first being introduced himself.

I was still wary of all of this, afraid that I sustained serious enough injuries to go crazy.

They waited.

"Um . . . Hi," I greeted them nervously.

"And your name?" Anna asked.

I hadn't realized that entities within my own head would need introductions. Didn't they already know all about the mind they were invading?

As I formulated these thoughts, they seemed to catch on, as if there was no emotion I could hide from them, which I guess made sense if they were projections of my own subconscious.

Anna, who seemed to be the calmest and collected of them all, tried to explain the situation to me. "We're not in your head."

I didn't understand, and I was too scared to try. My fear intensified as I thought of all the possibilities. Was I crazy? In the hospital? Where were my arms and my legs, and why couldn't I feel them? Surely, the crash must have paralyzed me. But still, there was nothing I could hide from these people.

"Please calm down," Anna pleaded. "Most people remember, but for some reason, you're having a bit of trouble. We can't explain what's going on if you don't calm down."

But I was in no state to calm down, and I didn't want to. I wanted my body back. I wanted the ability to move, to scream out to any doctor or nurse who might be outside the hospital room I was surely in, to run away from wherever I was, and to open my eyes and leave these beings who were invading the privacy of my mind.

My thoughts continued to run frantically, and I focused on getting away from wherever I was.

As my thoughts continued, the beings unrelentingly pleaded for me to calm down, but I simply couldn't. I was afraid, and I wanted to get back to Adam. At this point, he was the only thing that could calm me down. I wanted him to tell me that the last few minutes never happened and that I was dreaming.

Trying to escape from wherever I was, I removed myself from my efforts to communicate with these people, and I put myself in my happy place. I wanted to be gone, so I took my thoughts and put them elsewhere.

CHAPTER 4

I found myself in a memory I'd gone back to countless times. Whenever I felt down or sad, I turned back to this.

It was a few months after I first witnessed Adam's dazzling smile light up the library. After he had asked me out that Friday night, we'd been exclusively dating. For just over two months, Adam and I were practically inseparable when we weren't in class. Between classes, we would head to the college's food court together, and after class, we would hang out at one of our apartments, either watching movies or playing games. Most nights, we'd lay in bed telling secrets and life stories and laughing together.

This night was different. We were supposed to be

hanging out at Adam's apartment, but he wanted to go someplace alone and away from his roommate.

Adam surprised me by taking me out of town and down a dead-end road to a place I'd never been before. He called this place a hidden gem.

"Not many people know about this place," he told me. "It's the perfect time to come here because all the flowers are blooming."

The city was long behind us. We rode down the road with the windows down. The spring air was warm, and the sun was beginning to set. I stuck my hand out the window and played with the wind. Adam sat beside me in the driver's seat, looking as beautiful as ever.

As we made our way to the end of the road, I was anything but prepared for this type of beauty. Suddenly, we weren't in Illinois anymore. We weren't even on the same planet. The scene completely transformed, with beautiful green trees towering above us and stunning greenery and wildflowers blanketing the forest floor.

The road sloped down and around a bend to the left. We emerged out of the exquisite forest and into a clear opening. I noticed a field of grass first, but then I realized there was a small pond just beyond the meadow.

Adam parked the car, and we got out. Even though it was getting dark outside, I could still see the beauty of the area, and I stood there marveling at it. A sense of warmth overcame me just from being out in nature. The wind set the rhythm for the dancing blades of grass, and the crickets and frogs sang along.

Adam grabbed a blanket out of the back seat and spread it over the grass next to the pond. We lay there together, his arm around me and my head rested on his chest as we watched the sunset.

This moment was magical. I took the time to slow down my body and listen to the sounds of nature, feel the rise and fall of Adam's chest and his warmth around me, and watch the sun slowly creep toward the horizon.

With the stunning purples and pinks illuminating the sky, Adam turned to me, looked me in the eyes, and repeated my thoughts back to me.

"I love you," he told me for the first time.

"I love you, too," I replied genuinely.

He pulled me in closer and kissed the top of my forehead. We lay there silently for another few minutes, simply enjoying each other, before the sun finally set and the moon lit up the sky and sparkled off the nearby pond.

Adam finally broke the silence. "I know it sounds so stupid, but I've never said that to a girl."

"That's not stupid. I've never said that to a girl either," I joked.

He gave a giggle and nudged me, kissing me lightly on the lips to show that he approved of my humor.

He drew away, and his tone turned serious. "I was afraid of what you might say, which is why I've been so nervous to tell you."

"You don't have to worry anymore," I whispered.

I looked up at him and his beautiful eyes. Heat pooled deep in my belly, and everything about our encounter suddenly became intense. He grabbed the back of my head, put his other hand on the small of my back, and pulled me in close. His lips brushed mine passionately as my pulse quickened. He parted his lips, and we began to turn up the heat.

I crawled on top of him and straddled myself across his lap while keeping my lips pressed against his. My head spun as I took in his intoxicating scent. Adrenaline rushed throughout my veins as his hands moved all over me and his tongue danced around in my mouth. The hormones racing throughout my body must have done something to me; I'd never felt so confident in my life.

Joy, thrills, happiness, enjoyment, bliss, ecstasy. Every good emotion I'd ever encountered coursed through me all at once, unlike anything I'd ever felt before.

The butterflies once again sprang to life in my stomach, but this time, they spread through my entire body, fluttering through my veins and gathering between my thighs.

Adam's hands inched across my body, and he ran his fingers along the small of my back. As if he didn't know what else to do or unsure if he had permission, he continued rubbing the same spot on my back over and over. I took my right hand and grabbed his, guiding it downward.

If I thought what we were experiencing was some sort of huge flame in our passionate kissing, it grew even brighter as Adam grabbed ahold of my ass and pulled me even closer. I could feel how excited he was, and it only fueled my own excitement.

I came up for air as I grabbed the bottom of his shirt and pulled it up over his head. After a breath, I let myself fall right back to where I was, my lips once again glued to his. My hands trembled in excitement, and I ran them through his hair to calm my shaking body.

He slid his hands up my dress, running his fingers over my bare skin. My heart pounded quicker to match the tempo of his pulse, and I could hear both of our breathing patterns increase. It wasn't long before all our clothes were off and his hands were on my breasts, moving in rhythm with my racing heartbeat. This made the butterflies in my stomach transform into something else entirely, something unfamiliar yet comfortably thrilling.

Adam grabbed ahold of my body and flipped me over on my back as he climbed on top of me. He stopped for a second, looked at me, desire flaring in his eyes.

He was asking my permission with a single glance, and I gave a subtle nod. I already felt as if my heart was going to beat out of my chest, and my breathing rate increased to the point of near hyperventilation, but I craved more.

He pressed his body against mine. I wrapped my legs around his waist and pulled him in tight. There are no words that I could put to those feelings. Language can't describe the breathtaking astonishment and pleasure I felt in that moment. It was as if everything that had ever happened to me was leading up to this moment.

"I love you so much," I told him in between breaths.

"I love you, too," he whispered in my ear. "You're amazing."

Our bodies moved together until the moon was shining high above us. We fell onto the blanket beside each other, trying to catch our breath. Peace, pleasure, and comfort settled over me, and I knew with certainty that I was in love.

Once Adam caught his breath, he turned and looked me in the eye. "I've never done that with anyone before."

That stunned me. With his beautiful face and incredible charm, I found it hard to believe.

"What?" I asked in disbelief. "You must have girls all over you all the time."

"Not really," he admitted. "I'm not that good looking."

"I beg to differ," I argued. Did he really believe this?

"I mean, girls like me, and I've had girlfriends," he continued, "but I've never found one that I care enough about. I'm just glad I found you." He twisted his head to look at me, and his eyes glistened with tender affection.

"I wasn't planning for this to happen," he admitted.

I tangled my fingers in his. "I'm glad it did."

"Me, too." He smiled, but his eyes caught something near my head. "That's a pretty rock."

He picked it up and held it so both of us could see. It was jagged on one side, with pretty orange and gray swirls all over its surface.

"You should keep it," I told him. "Then every time you look at it, you'll think of me."

Adam smiled. "I'm always thinking of you. Perhaps I'll have to start a collection."

"We can start one together," I offered. I liked the idea of building something with him—whether it was a rock collection or our lives. I just wanted us to be together.

"Together," he repeated.

We sat in silence again, still working to catch our breath.

"We really must be losers if we waited until nineteen to do anything like this," I joked.

"No," he informed me. "Not losers. Just very, very lucky. And in love."

He tucked his hands under his head and looked up at the stars. I moved my head onto his chest and pulled a corner of the blanket over us.

"In love," I repeated, *really focusing on the word.* Yes, I *thought.* This feels perfect.

It *was* a perfect moment, which is why I found myself going back to it so often. I had played the entire night over in my head time and time again after it occurred, and it quickly became so familiar and unforgettable to me. I'd memorized every detail and feeling.

But now that the memory was over, I had to return to the voices in my head. By now, I was calmed down after working my way through my happiest memory.

"Can we talk now?" one of the beings asked.

It was like my memory really did take me to a new place where they couldn't access it. They didn't show any sign that they witnessed the details.

"I suppose," I replied. "I'd really like to know why you're here."

"Your situation is unusual," Anna began to explain. "We don't get many, but it happens. I'm going to start with the simplest explanation, and we'll go from there. How do I put this in words that you'll understand?"

Then another person—Darryl, I think—stepped in. "You're dead."

Suddenly, any calmness I was feeling vanished, and I transitioned from trying to understand the situation to getting plain furious.

First, I was certain there was no afterlife. Second, if

there was one, I was upset that someone would present it to me in such a blunt way. Third—and most devastating of all—if I really was dead, that meant I would never see Adam again. My heart seemed to shatter into a million pieces all at once.

"Dead!?" I threw my emotions at them. "But I'm still here! I can't be dead."

For a moment, I believed that I was just in a coma. Perhaps my mind was still playing tricks on me.

I tried to find my eyes so the tears could spring to life, but I didn't know where they were. I searched for that familiar ache in my chest, but there was no physical pain. Yet that hurt, betrayed, and frustrated feeling that comes with breaking down was still there. I felt like I was going to burst, and in some odd sense that I couldn't pinpoint, it almost felt *good*. It was somewhat of a relief that I was feeling *something* and that I wasn't completely gone.

On second that, I wasn't sure this was a good thing.

It's better to feel pain than nothing at all. That's what I've heard people say, but I didn't know if I wanted to believe that. If there was no chance that I'd be with Adam again, I think I'd rather not exist.

Gone. I couldn't grasp the concept that I was actually gone, outside my own body, and that I would never feel the thrills once associated with a physical body again. I couldn't imagine never seeing Adam again.

My mind is playing tricks on me, I tried to rationalize with myself. *I'm still here. I still exist. I'm just badly injured.*

The entities around me tried to help again, but I couldn't listen to them. I wanted to go back to Adam. I wanted to wake up from whatever coma I was in. I wanted to feel his touch like I had that night by the pond. I wanted to feel his lips on mine and know that I was safe.

The voices in my head threw unrelenting emotions of urgency at me, but I tried to ignore them. I struggled to understand what thoughts were racing through my head separate from theirs.

"Adam!" I wanted to call his name. I searched for my eyes again and tried to open them, but once again, I was unsuccessful.

Then very distantly, I heard a voice calling out to me —a voice this time, not just a thought.

A real voice.

A familiar voice.

Adam's voice.

"Liz!" he called out. There was sorrow, sadness, and pain behind his voice. "Liz, oh God, I am so sorry. Please don't leave!"

Adam! I tried shouting. *Adam, I'm right here. Oh God, please hear me. I'm not gone!*

Adam called out to me one last time as I reached my hardest toward the voice and strained to connect with him.

Suddenly, I found my eyes, and they shot open.

CHAPTER 5

I wasn't expecting this. I thought I was paralyzed and couldn't feel anything. For a moment, I actually believed I might be dead. When I opened my eyes, though, the most excruciating pain raced through my body.

Adam hovered over me, panic filling his eyes. "Liz, oh my God!"

I could see that he wanted to touch me, but he was afraid. Judging by the pain expanding throughout me, it was because he didn't want to hurt me any more than I was already injured.

As I tried to force my eyes open even more and see past my dizziness, I discovered we were still in the folded-up vehicle. Only seconds had passed since we hit the tree. Blood ran down Adam's face, and his right pointer finger was severely distorted.

Broken, I thought.

Most of the windows had shattered out, and icy-cold air rushed across my skin. It looked as if the side of Adam's face took the blow of the driver's side window. The airbags had gone off, but that was all I could process. It took all I had to focus on Adam's face, and it was the only thing I wanted to look at.

I tried to speak, to tell him I loved him, but all that came out was a simple squeak. It was loud enough for him to perk up a little with hope.

"Come on, babe, open your eyes," he begged in a broken tone. "I'm here."

I couldn't. There was so much pain that I couldn't move or hardly think. I tried my best to reach out to him with my thoughts and tell him I loved him in case I didn't make it, but I couldn't find my way past the agony.

It was then that I felt myself slipping again. Everything began turning black as the pain started to fade away. I tried to whisper a goodbye. I was sure this was it now. I was sinking off into nonexistence.

I clawed my way back to consciousness and forced my eyes open. I vowed to push past the pain and spend any last few seconds I had savoring the moment with Adam. Any second now, I was sure everything would turn black and there wouldn't be any more thoughts racing around my head. There wouldn't be voices or memories in there, because that's what death was. Death was nonexistence, and the darkness never ended.

Adam continued to reach for hope, believing his voice would keep me there. "Please, Liz. Please. I need you. I'm so sorry. I need you."

Tears streamed down his face, mixing with the blood that was dripping from the gash across the left side of his forehead.

"Remember…" I whispered, trying to formulate words. It was one of the toughest things I'd ever done.

Adam went silent, trying to let me speak. "Yes," he prompted after a few seconds. "Yes, keep talking. I'm right here."

"Remember…" I was having trouble making any noise. "The pond? Your hidden gem?"

"Of course I remember," he told me, rubbing his finger across my forehead and back through my hair. "It was the most magical experience of my life. More exciting than your twenty-first birthday."

We both liked looking back on that, and we recalled it as one of our craziest memories. As crazy as we were that night, we still loved talking about how amazing and thrilling it was. Maybe this was the type of thing my father was talking about when he said Adam had changed me.

Neither of us had ever been crazy people. I was raised a good girl. I got good grades and never went out partying. Hell, I didn't even have a date to prom. There was nothing special about my high school years.

When I met Adam, all the little things I never got to experience about high school finally became reality. We started sneaking around like we were teenagers with a curfew. Desperate for some of those high school thrills, we'd occasionally park our car in a secluded lot at night and get it on in the back seat. We'd sometimes even walk along some of the hiking trails outside of town and find a great bench to make love on under the moonlight.

That was about as crazy as things got for us. We'd never done drugs or anything illegal, and we pretty much kept to ourselves.

The night of my twenty-first birthday was different. I was turning twenty-one. I thought that was as good of an excuse as any to let everything go and get a little crazy. I wanted to throw myself away for the night and become a different Liz. I wanted to let the party animal out. So together, we let ourselves go.

That night, we headed out to the bars with our friends to get wasted. Walking hand in hand with Adam on my left and Shae on my right, I jumped up and down in excitement. Shae was dating Adam's roommate, Cody.

Cody hung on to Shae's other hand. Shae was my best friend right after my dad and Adam, although she wasn't anything like me. She wore dark makeup and had a full tattoo sleeve running up her right arm. It was odd how well we got along, but somehow, we connected by talking about books— she enjoyed fantasy novels—and dishing our feelings about our boyfriends.

When we entered the bar, I was ready to have some fun. Shae pulled out a sash from her purse and sang Happy Birthday to me as she slid it over my head. The sash read Birthday Girl, and for once in my life, I was having fun being the center of attention.

Tonight, I didn't care who was watching. It was my turn to go crazy, and as much as I believed I'd regret it later, I knew there would be great stories to tell by the end of the night.

"Let's get this girl a whiskey!" Cody shouted.

The bartender grabbed a shot glass and set it on the counter.

"No, no, no," I refused, stopping him in his tracks. "Do you have something fruity?"

"Not tonight, birthday girl," Cody told me. "You're not going to have any fun with a hard lemonade."

"Yes, I will," I protested. "If I drink enough."

I looked at Adam for support. "Whatever you want, babe."

I sat there for a moment but decided I was prepared to try anything. "Fine, but you better find me something good."

"Oh, it'll be good," Cody promised.

After Cody ordered a drink I wasn't familiar with, the bartender set a shot in front of me. My friends cheered me on, but it took a moment to prepare myself.

"Here it goes." I tilted my head back quickly and let the drink flow to the back of my throat. It burned as it went down, but I swallowed it successfully. My nose crinkled.

"That awful, was it?" Adam asked.

"Yes. That awful." After a moment, I wiped the disgust off my face and replaced it with a smile. "Let's get another one!"

The night went on like that. People bought me drinks, I graciously accepted, and I even hit the dance floor with Shae.

It didn't take long before I started feeling sick. I didn't even think I had that much to drink. I could still walk without needing support, but I wasn't myself anymore.

Adam noticed how ill I was becoming and kindly took me out the back door of the bar. He held my hair as I puked in the alley. After I was done, I leaned my back against the outside wall and slid down until I was sitting on the ground.

The hysterics hit me a moment later. I laughed gleefully and started singing.

Adam sat beside me and laughed along with me, and we

were having a carefree time. I was loudly singing when I suddenly stopped.

"Hey!" I cried. Adam jumped at the sound of my voice. "Let's do something even crazier."

"I don't think you're in any state for that," Adam laughed.

"Spontaneous! Let's do something completely stupid. After all, it's my birthday. It's like I have a license to do stupid things."

I stood up, stumbling a bit, grabbed Adam's hand, and held on to him as we started walking. "I wanna be spontaneous. Let's do something we'll regret," I sang to a made-up tune as I skipped along.

We walked for a while holding on to each other and basking in our ridiculousness, having the time of our lives. We no longer knew where we were, and we didn't care that our friends had no idea where we were, either. We walked along the sidewalk with just a few streetlamps illuminating the night. There weren't any cars driving nearby.

A fence bordered the sidewalk, enclosing a private building. Caution signs were posted around the fence, and with as much fun as I was having, we were about halfway along the length of the fence before I realized this.

"I found our something stupid," I informed Adam.

The building beyond the fence looked like a school. It was made of brick and had window-shaped holes in the side, although there was no glass in them. Construction supplies were scattered everywhere. It looked as if they were getting ready to tear the building down and were salvaging some of it. I started to climb the fence, which wasn't very tall, and crashed to the other side.

"What are you doing?" Adam hissed.

I was already over the fence and headed for the abandoned school. "Being crazy," I said, turning back to him.

Adam followed over the fence and ran toward me. We crawled in through one of the holes where a window once sat. I found my way into one of the classrooms, which was empty now.

"What do you think about me being a teacher?" I asked as I stood in front of the room and mimicked a teacher's stance, pointing to space on the wall where the chalk board used to be.

"I think you'd be great," Adam told me as he took his seat in one of the old desks that was sitting in the corner. Most of them had been removed, and the ones that remained were covered in a thick layer of dust.

He raised his hand.

"Yes?" I called on him as a teacher would.

"Ms. Janssen, I have a question."

"Yes, Mr. Loveless, what's your question?" I replied, trying to be all proper while attempting to hold in my giggles.

"Are student-teacher relationships appropriate at this school?"

I pretended to think about it for a second. "Technically, no, but I'll make an exception for you."

I swung my leg over the desk, as if I was getting on a horse, and straddled myself over him.

"For you, I'll gladly make an exception," I whispered.

I took his face in my hands and kissed him hard on the lips.

"Now let's explore!" I tried to quickly get off the desk but stumbled along the way, probably a bit more clumsily than I would admit.

We walked down the empty hallways, and I went along dizzily, trying to maintain my footing. At the end of the hall-way, we found a set of stairs that went down into the basement.

"Let's go see what lies down here," I challenged him.

We descended the stairs and attempted to look around, but it was pitch black. Since there was nothing to see, Adam grabbed ahold of me, pressed me against a nearby wall, and crashed his lips into mine. My hands found their way beneath his waistband as he moved his hands up my shirt.

"This would probably be the craziest place we've ever done it," I told him.

"Mm... right here?" he teased, trailing hot kisses down my neck.

Something squeaked, and we both went rigid. The sound of

scurrying footsteps met my ears, and I squealed. "Never mind!"

I was not getting it on in some rat-infested basement.

Adam grabbed my hand protectively, and we raced back up the stairs. When we reached the top, we heard a faint click, and then a light shone directly at us. I threw my hand up to shield my eyes.

"Hey!" someone shouted.

"Shit," Adam whispered. "Run!"

Before I had time to process what was going on, Adam had jumped headfirst out the hole in the wall next to us and had rolled on the grass. Without a second thought, I followed him out the first-story window and raced after him.

My heart beat like crazy, and adrenaline raced through my system. It felt thrilling to run away from the police. My mind was having a hard time processing morals, and all I knew was that it was one of the most frightening, exciting, and exhilarating moments of my life.

"The Fuzz! The Fuzz!" Adam shouted.

I saw the police car parked on the side of the road, and I knew any good girl would stop and pay punishment for her crime, but I simply didn't care. I was letting all the crazy out.

I ran as fast as I could after Adam and somehow managed to make my way over the fence despite how disoriented I was. We took off running down the street, but it didn't take long to lose the cop. He must have not been in very good shape for me to outrun him in my state.

Out of breath, we stopped when we were sure we were no longer being followed.

"Holy shit!" I breathed.

"Holy shit is right," Adam agreed.

My heart continued racing, and I fought to catch my breath. My adrenaline levels sank slowly, but I was still far from normal. Adam let out a slight giggle, which made me laugh, and then we both went into a full on laughing fit.

"Shit," Adam said once he caught his breath. "Well, that was exciting!"

And it was. We weren't about to do it again anytime soon, but the memory was something only we shared together, and we cherished it for that.

After it all was over, we often joked about that night.

Adam would say things like, "Liz, don't ever turn twenty-one again."

I would scold him for, "Running away from me like that."

If the night did anything for us, it brought us closer together and showed us some of the rollercoaster-like thrills that we'd never experienced before.

It was a cherished memory that took all bad emotions—fright, danger, terror, and anxiety—and rolled them into something good—a bonding experience, an adventure, and a memory. That's why we loved it so much.

Back in the car, the clock was still ticking, and I knew I only had moments left. I could hardly keep my eyes open anymore, and I was having even more trouble controlling my lips. The tears in my eyes sprang to life and fell fast down my face. It felt good knowing that I could find my eyes this time and that I wasn't completely gone yet.

But the darkness was still coming. Darkness, it felt, because I was going numb, but there was also a light coming at me. My first thought was headlights, but that didn't seem right.

Maybe, I thought for a split second, *this is the light I'm supposed to go into.*

Knowing I only had seconds left, minutes at the most, I tried to speak quickly, but it was incredibly difficult with the pain shooting out from the right side of my head. I could barely move my lips or produce any sound from my throat.

"Please…" I rasped. "Don't forget me."

"I won't, Liz," Adam promised. "I could never do that."

"When… when I'm gone, I want someone to remember me. I never had a… a chance… to make an… impact."

"Don't say that," Adam scolded. "You're the most important person in my life, and you made an impact on *me*."

"Promise me… that you'll find someone else and be happy."

My thoughts turned back to my father's depression, and all I knew was that I didn't want Adam mourning over me like that for so long. I wanted him happy, even though somewhere within my heart, I wanted him to only be *mine*. But he couldn't, not if I was going to leave this soon.

"You're not going to die!" he assured me. "If you do, we'll be together again. I promise!"

I tried to scoff, but the pain was too unbearable. *Him and his ridiculous beliefs*, I thought.

The light intensified, pulling me in, and I struggled to assure myself there was nothing beyond that, to inspire myself to make the best of these last few moments. Once I let it completely engulf me, all my thoughts and memories would be gone forever.

I tried to believe him. I really did, but it just didn't sound possible.

"Don't make promises you can't keep," I told him.

"I love you, and I promise you that I always will. That's a promise I can and will keep. I *know* we'll be together again."

My eyes could barely see a clear image, and the pain was starting to fade. I was leaving.

"I love you, too," I said to him one last time, and then that beautiful face faded away into nothing.

It was over.

For a moment, I was gone. Everything was colorless, painless, and nonexistent, but then I became aware again, back inside my head where I had found those others before.

I wasn't dead yet.

CHAPTER 6

I was no longer engulfed in a colorless, painless, thoughtless state. That only lasted a moment, a split second when I was nowhere. Gone.

But then I woke up. It wasn't blackness, because there was no sense of color here. If anything, it was a bright and misty place. Bright because it was just the opposite of the darkness. In the dark, I was simply gone. Here, I was aware, and that gave me a sense of relief in a way. Misty because it was so *confusing*. It was hard to see past myself.

When I became aware again, I knew I was in the same place I'd been before, the place where I met those three voices. But I was still completely lost. I was sure I was dead now. I knew I wouldn't make it past that excruciating pain. But I didn't understand how I was still so aware of my surroundings.

I guess I was wrong, I thought. *Adam was right. There is a heaven.*

"No, not Heaven." Someone shared their thoughts with me. Anna, I think it was based on my previous encounter.

I was still frightened, not knowing what to expect, but I wanted my questions answered, and I was willing to open my mind a bit to what those answers might be.

"Okay," I thought to the woman, taking a moment to relax. "I'm ready to talk."

I paused my thoughts for a moment before adding, "I think."

I now felt two entities connecting with me, and based on what I remembered, it felt like Anna and Eric, the two people who introduced themselves earlier.

"What happened to the other guy?" I asked them.

"He was having trouble understanding your situation," Eric replied. "We sent him away."

I didn't care that he had left. I was ready for some answers. I started out slowly, really trying to understand what my *situation* was.

"I may be stubborn, but I'm not stupid," I started. "I was dead for a moment before, then?"

"In a sense of the word *dead*," Anna told me. "Yes, you were dead."

"Am I dead now?" I knew the answer to that question, but I needed confirmation.

"Yes. Well . . . not dead, really. I mean, there is no death in the way you're thinking, but I suppose. I mean, you can't go back to your old life." It seemed Anna was having a hard time explaining it to me, and I was still very lost.

"But I did go back," I reminded her.

"Well, yeah…" She seemed confused herself. "That's not really supposed to happen."

"What is this?" I demanded. "Heaven?"

"Sort of." It was Eric who gave this thought this time.

"Let's call it an afterlife," Anna explained. "It's not Heaven because there's no creator here."

"What is it then?" I asked. "Don't you have experience explaining this to people like me, people who have just died?"

Anna seemed a little taken aback. "Well, no. Normally we just welcome them back and we don't have to explain anything."

I didn't understand. Why was I different? Why was it all so confusing?

"Most people remember," she informed me.

"Why don't I remember?" I demanded.

Despite my confusion and hopefulness for some answers, my thoughts were still turning back to Adam. I saw his bloody face and tear-filled eyes fade away in my mind, and I tried to keep his beautiful eyes and cute dimple fresh in my thoughts. It was difficult to focus on him and my *situation* at the same time.

I could tell Anna was trying to formulate her thoughts carefully as she worked on responding to my question. "Because there's something keeping you from remembering… emotionally."

Adam, I thought. *I love him so much, and I don't want to leave him. I'd rather be with him forever and never remember anything than to be without him.*

I took my thoughts and ran with them, hoping to keep my most valued memories, the ones I shared with Adam. I didn't want to forget anything about his beauty, personality, or love for me.

I frantically flipped through my memories. I took myself back to the moment we met. I visualized the first time we kissed, and I attempted to burn the taste of his lips in my mind. Each thought passed through my mind like a quick snapshot of every moment as if I were playing the memories on a slideshow.

I took myself back to the pond, but this time I was already familiar with it, and we were several years older.

"Adam, what are we doing here?" I asked.

"Shh," he quieted me. He led me out of the vehicle and kissed my lips softly. His hands gently gripped my biceps, and he looked into my eyes seriously. "Liz..."

"What's going on?" I asked suspiciously. "You're acting weird."

"That's because I'm nervous," he admitted.

I furrowed my brow. "Nervous about what?"

"Shh," he quieted me again. "Just . . . don't say anything until I'm done. Okay?"

"Okay," I agreed.

"I said don't say anything." He smiled playfully, then took a deep breath. "Liz, I've loved you for a long time. I swear to God I loved you before I even met you."

He had me smiling already, but I still wasn't catching on.

"I love everything about you. I love your smile and your hair and your gorgeous blue eyes. I think it's cute the way your nose is always stuck in a book, and I love that we have so much in common, and I don't just mean the obvious like that we're both nurses. I love that you're honest and you're nice. You never say anything bad about anyone, and you always look on the positive side of everything."

I appreciated the compliments, but I still wasn't sure where this was going.

"That's the kind of person I want to spend the rest of my life with," he said with a genuine smile as he reached in his *pocket. Then he knelt to the ground and presented me with an open box.*

I took a small step back as my eyes went wide, and I threw my hands over my dropped jaw. I was overwhelmed with emotion as I finally understood what was going on. My heart pumped vigorously, and tears began welling up in my eyes, not because I was nervous or scared or sad, but because I was overcome with joy and happiness. Those butterflies once again came to life, and it took me a few moments to catch my breath.

"Elizabeth Marie Janssen," he continued. My heart rate increased, and my eyes became damp as I waited for him to finish so I could give him my answer. "Will you do the great honor of spending the rest of your life with me?"

"Yes, yes, yes!" I shouted as I flung myself on him and wrapped my arms around his neck. "Yes, I will marry you," I confirmed as I planted a passionate kiss on his lips.

Adam wrapped his arms around my waist and stood up, bringing me with him. He set me down and grabbed the ring from the box. I stuck out my hand and let him place the delicate white gold ring on my left ring finger.

I hugged him again. "Yes, I will marry you!"

My memories didn't end there, and they weren't always happy ones, but they all included Adam. The next snapshot was of our first fight, the one where we tried debating over religion before ultimately deciding that we wouldn't let our beliefs tear apart our love.

The next memory that flashed by was the time I told Adam I couldn't have kids. It was shortly after the first time we made love. I had been contemplating how I would tell him for a while, but I could never work up the courage or find a good time.

The time struck when we were cuddling on his couch, just the two of us, watching a movie.

Out of the blue, Adam asked, "Do you think I could have gotten you pregnant? I mean, we didn't use protection." He was clearly worried, and his own anxiety I'm sure had been holding him back from asking the question.

Nerves began welling up inside of me. My heart rate increased, and my hands became sweaty. I knew I had to tell him now. It wasn't fair not to, but I was afraid that if I did, he wouldn't want me anymore.

"Look, Adam..." I started with difficulty.

"Yeah?" he asked with no indication of a shift in emotions.

"I... I don't know how to say this."

"Oh, God, you're pregnant?" Adam's eyes filled with terror. "I want kids, Liz, but not now."

"No, no!" I protested quickly. I grew more nervous, and my heart was pumping so hard I was sure he could hear it by now. I was so afraid to tell him, scared that he might break up

with me because of it. "I would love kids, too. It's just..." I took a deep breath. "I can't."

"Oh," Adam said in a simple manner. He didn't press the issue farther. He just left it at that and looked back at the TV. He wrapped his arms around me a little tighter and kissed me on the top of my forehead.

My nerves lightened, and my heart rate recessed to normal. I was shocked at how well he was taking it, but I think he could see how much it bothered me. I don't think I'd ever been more nervous than that moment when I almost believed he would leave me because of something I couldn't control. I eventually told him about my past and why my illness left me infertile, and it didn't seem to bother him.

"I'd rather have you without kids than have kids with someone else," he'd told me.

"If I could, I'd do whatever it took to give you children," I promised.

"There are other options if it's something we really want," Adam suggested.

I liked that idea, but it still pained me to know I couldn't do it on my own.

The memory passed quickly, and then they continued. I shifted through my most memorable experiences with him, desperate to hold on to every emotion we ever shared, not willing to let go of my few short years with him.

I used each memory to fuel my calls back out to him. Maybe if I called back again, I could make it back to my body and hold on until the EMTs arrive.

"Adam!" I called out. "I don't want to be without you."

"You can be with him again," Anna informed me cautiously. "You just have to wait until he… dies… and comes here. Then you can go back together."

Wait? I didn't want to wait. I didn't want to spend a second without him.

I had gone back before. I could do it again. I reached out once more. I held on to my favorite memories—the first time we met, when we drove down by the pond, when Adam proposed—and I called out to him.

Behind my thoughts, I could tell Anna was sending warnings, begging me not to do this, but I didn't care. I couldn't wait for him to live out his life without me. With everything we'd been through, that just wasn't fair. If I could go back once, I could do it again, and maybe I could hold on long enough for my body to heal.

I continued reaching, playing back through my memories, calling out his name, reaching further and further into my thoughts until I heard him calling back. It was faint at first, a cry of pain and sorrow, but I held on to it as tight as I could, and I drew myself toward the voice, toward real words. I could feel myself slowly making my way back to him as the volume of his voice grew.

"Liz!" He was yelling now, and his voice was full of pain. I didn't have to see his face to know that his tear ducts were working as hard as a broken faucet. He cried out one more time, louder this time. "Elizabeth!"

Colors burst across my vision. Suddenly, I could see again, and I was back in the car.

But my eyes didn't open like last time. I could see that. I also saw Adam clinging onto my unmoving body, crying over me.

I was sitting in the back seat, looking over it all, outside of my own body.

CHAPTER 7

I watched the scene from the back seat. Adam's face was drenched in tears, and his body was draped over mine, hugging me and clinging to my unmoving form.

From this perspective, my injuries looked incredibly painful, and this sight now clearly explained the excruciating pain I felt just moments ago. Blood cascaded down my face and soaked into my clothing, and small pieces of glass stuck out of my exposed skin. My silky straight hair was tangled and coated in fluid. How did I survive for any length of time looking like that?

Snow whizzed past the windows, and Adam continued speaking to my body. "There's so much I never got to say to you. I—I..."

He wept, but he had to take a deep breath before he

could speak again. "I was saving it for our vows. If you can still hear me, if you're still out there, I want you to know how much I love you. I never told you this, but when we first met, I was scared to death."

I was struck with surprise. He never showed any indication of nerves. He always seemed so confident.

"I saw you in the library, and for a brief instant, I thought I knew you from somewhere. I tried placing you, but then I realized we had never met. You were just so beautiful." His breath wavered. "I saw you studying, and I thought I should just leave you alone. You probably didn't want to be bothered."

He took a deep breath again, sniffling in between words. "But then I thought, *This girl looks so lonely, yet there's surely something special about her.* I couldn't pass up my chance to meet you. I knew that if I didn't introduce myself then, I'd never get to know you."

He squeezed his eyes shut, and tears streamed down his cheeks. "I took a few moments to really look at you, and then I walked up to you. I was so nervous. You seemed to take the introduction so easily."

What? Did he really believe this? My mind raced with thoughts, touched by what he was saying and completely surprised.

"I never in a million years thought that I would meet

someone like you. I always thought that God brought us together for a reason. But WHY?"

He screamed the word *why* loudly with a strong sense of agony behind it and a hint of frustration. If I still had a heart, it would have skipped a beat and made me jump.

"Why would he take you away now?" He shook his head and took a few moments to sob before continuing, this time in a slow, quiet tone. "I thought I was there to help you or something. I mean, you'd been through so much. I always had it so easy, but I really started believing that God brought us together because *I* needed *you*. You're such a great person, and you made me see the world in a whole new light. I'm not ready to let you go. The world still needs you and the beautiful, magical light you bring to it."

Adam began sobbing again and lowered his head, pressing his forehead against my shoulder. The tears streamed down his face even harder now.

I hadn't noticed until now that there were other cars stopped behind ours. A line of vehicles—surely families heading home from Christmas service—were parked along the road. All I could see through the thick snowfall were pairs of dim lights.

No one had come to check on us yet. How long had

it been since our vehicle caught a sheet of ice and skidded into the ditch? Minutes, I guessed.

Someone in one of the stopped vehicles must have called the ambulance since they arrived just moments later. I heard the sirens before I could see the flashing lights through the blizzard.

Someone made their way to the vehicle—it looked like an EMT through the darkness. Adam clung to my body as the EMTs tried to get us out of the vehicle to inspect our injuries.

I was focusing on Adam too much to look at what the paramedics were doing to my body or to the vehicle. They were trying to coax Adam out of the car and nearly had to pry him off of me. He was in too much agony to really fight it, I think, because as he cried and reached for me, he still allowed the paramedics to place a neck brace on him. He was freely following their procedures, while actively trying to fight them off.

As his body lost contact with mine, he cried even harder, screaming my name as he left the vehicle. He limped away, still crying out for me. The paramedics settled him into a stretcher.

Despite how much he wanted to hang on to me, I think he understood it was no use. He was in too much pain—both physically and emotionally—to try too hard to fight the paramedics off.

I wanted to touch him and speak to him. I wanted to tell him that I heard what he was saying. The way he was shouting my name scared me.

I wanted to follow him. I tried grabbing the door handle from the back seat, but my hands wouldn't take a hold of it. I was stunned with confusion for a moment before I remembered my dead body sitting just feet from me.

Of course, I thought.

Instead of trying to open the door, I simply pushed my way through it without a problem and stepped out of the vehicle.

Even though I had long since relinquished the idea of an afterlife and didn't surrender to the idea of the supernatural, I couldn't deny the fact any longer. I was clearly dead, and there was no going back to the body that once housed my spirit. I'd worked in nursing homes and hospitals long enough to know what a dead body looked like.

But I didn't care about my body. That's not what mattered to me. What mattered to me was Adam, and I had to make sure he was alright.

Snow crashed to the ground, and the wind blew it across the road in quick, strong gusts. It was dark out, and the people who had stopped to spectate were wrapped in tight winter jackets, earmuffs, and gloves. Most of their noses were turning red from the cold.

When I stepped out of the vehicle and into the snow, the cold didn't hit me like I expected it to. In fact, I didn't feel cold at all. I didn't feel anything. I couldn't feel the wind on my face, the cold biting at my cheeks, or even my own feet on the ground.

I walked away from the vehicle towards the flashing lights, where Adam was being tended to by paramedics.

I took a moment to look back to where I had come from. There weren't any footprints leading to where I stood. I could see the EMTs gently trying to pry my body from the car, although we all knew it was a lost cause. I was already gone.

I walked to the back of the ambulance, where Adam was struggling and fighting each touch of the paramedics. I didn't think he was trying to combat them off. I think he was trying to fight away his emotional strife. He was still sobbing my name loudly.

I wanted to comfort him and tell him I was right here, but I couldn't get near him. Several EMTs were trying to hold him down while another attempted to lightly dress the wound on his head. Yet another was examining his broken finger.

I was close enough to see him now, but there were so

many people surrounding him that there was no way I could touch him. I came even closer, hoping to get a better glimpse of what the EMTs were doing to him. No one tried pushing me away or telling me he needed his space. No one even looked up at me. They simply continued about their business without a single indication of my presence.

As I neared the crowd of medical professionals and came almost close enough to immerse myself in the group, one of the paramedics turned away from the rest, clearly on a mission. Her eyes gazed past me, and she took a quick step and landed directly where I was standing. She was moving too fast for me to get out of the way. Without skipping a beat, she continued on her way, determined to fulfill her mission.

Did we just occupy the same space for a moment? I thought I saw her shiver, but I took it as a sign of the chilly weather.

By this time, word of the accident had already spread throughout the line of cars and back up toward the church. I watched as Adam's parents, along with a few of his other relatives, raced down the road toward the ambulance in a panic.

Sue's face filled with horror as she rounded the ambulance doors. She saw Adam and came to an abrupt halt, nearly crashing to the ground. At the same time, her features suddenly shifted. Tears instantly streamed down her face, and she began bawling.

"Adam, thank Heavens you're okay." She flung herself toward him, but he didn't even notice she was there. He was still calling out my name in anguish.

The way Adam was struggling yet not pushing the EMTs away was odd to me. It was like he knew that this was the procedure and the way it needed to go, yet he was fighting *himself* to not escape the stretcher and run back to my body.

Two EMTs tried to push Sue back. "He needs his space, ma'am," a man told her as he gently placed a hand on her chest and guided her away from the crowd.

She attempted to push her way past him, more fiercely now, but the EMT had his arms around her and was trying to keep her away from him.

"My baby!" she cried.

She stopped struggling for a moment, looked the EMT straight in the eyes, and shouted, "That's my son, God dammit!" She then began aggressively fighting his tight grip again.

The man strained to calm her down as Jim stepped in, eyes full of sorrow, and hugged his wife from behind, attempting to soothe her.

As soon as her husband touched her, her whole body

went limp, and she began shaking, sobbing into the EMT's shoulder as Jim stroked her hair. They led her away from the ambulance and worked on comforting her sobs.

Adam was still kicking and screaming my name, but there were too many EMTs holding him down for him to get anywhere. I watched as the lady returned and stuck a needle in his arm. He slowly went limp, his screaming ceased, and they were finally able to tend to his injuries properly.

"Let's get this man to the hospital," one of them said.

Together, they hoisted his limp body into the ambulance as some of them piled in the back and others went to the front. Without a second thought, I jumped in the back of the vehicle just as they slammed the doors.

Finally, enough people had scattered so that I could get close to him. It was crowded in the back of the ambulance, but I was able to stand there without a problem.

No one paid any indication to my presence, and in just a few moments, the ambulance was on its way, taking it slow as to not cause another accident.

"He's pretty banged up, but he'll be alright," one of the EMTs assured the other.

Adam had an open wound on his forehead and a broken finger. I took note of that before, but I hadn't realized the other bruises that were forming across the rest of his body. Big purple splotches covered his face, and other injuries lay patterned across his body. I was certain he had whiplash, too.

Adam was still somewhat aware, still mumbling my name while rolling his eyes back and forth in his head.

There was nothing I could do but observe. I knew if I touched him, nothing would come about from it, but I tried anyway. I couldn't resist getting near my heartbroken fiancé.

My hand touched his, but I couldn't feel any physical contact. For a brief moment, I thought I saw a change in his features. It appeared as if his hand twitched, and his mumblings stopped for an instant. I almost believed he could feel my touch, but another second later, he was back to mumbling my name.

We reached the hospital, and the doors opened again. Everyone shuttered as the cold air raced into the back of the vehicle. Again, I didn't feel anything.

I jumped out of the back and waited for the paramedics to bring Adam. Within seconds, they were out of the vehicle and headed through the hospital doors. I followed them down the hospital corridors and observed as they further inspected Adam's wounds.

I observed as the doctors leaned over Adam's nearly still form until all the personnel dissipated. With the blizzard, they had hordes of injuries to tend to. I didn't know where my body was or what was happening to it, and I didn't care.

When they stepped away, the blood that was covering Adam's body not long ago was gone, replaced by more purple splotches underneath. He was held together by bandages and gauze, but I knew he was going to recover. I'd seen much worse.

Adam and I were left alone behind the curtains. I didn't know how long this would last. He'd become more aware by now and was lying there quietly staring at the ceiling, his eyes unmoving. I could see the loss and grief in his eyes. He knew he had lost me, and he was probably playing it back through his head, trying to make sense of it all.

I hadn't tried speaking since I came back in this unusual, non-physical form. I could see my hands, and I could hear people bustling by the room, but I couldn't smell anything, and I couldn't feel anything. All I could do was observe, like I was watching a television show, rather than actually experiencing it.

With impaired senses, I wasn't sure if my voice would actually work. It wasn't difficult to find my lips, not like it had been when I was completely detached in the white mist. I tried to make contact with Adam's hand, and I was able to croak out the words, "I love you."

Since no one could see me or feel me, I was sure no

one could hear me, either. Just as I was thinking this, believing that Adam wouldn't hear my voice, I watched as his eyes jerked towards me and stared directly into me. Not through me like the EMTs and doctors had done. But *at me*. Right into my eyes.

The grief and pain in his eyes immediately disappeared, and they unexpectedly lit up with joy.

I was taken by surprise, and all my notions of the state I was in came crashing down. Adam didn't look through me the way the rest of the hospital personnel did. He *saw* me.

I was taken so off guard that I suddenly wasn't holding on to him anymore. Everything I was observing abruptly disappeared. All my remaining senses left me simultaneously.

I found myself back in the white mist once again.

CHAPTER 8

"What were you thinking!?" Anna scolded me like a child who just ran out into the street, pressing upon all disappointment, fear, and anger she could muster.

"Adam," I thought. "I need to get back to Adam. He saw me. He *saw* me."

I was frantic. All I could think about was Adam and getting back to him. My thoughts raced, replaying the way he looked at me. He *knew* I was there.

Anna and Eric shoved their thoughts and emotions at me. Anna pressed thoughts of caution at me while Eric used some type of calming technique to soothe my emotions.

I didn't listen. I couldn't. I was too absorbed in the

last few seconds that I couldn't understand much of what was going on.

"I went back twice now. I can do it again," I told myself as I began calling out once more in an attempt to return.

I couldn't mask my desperation. Anna continued throwing thoughts of caution at me. Then suddenly, her emotions flamed. Something burst inside of her, and she fired those blazing ideas at me fiercely.

It felt like the one and only time my mother had ever slapped me. I had run out into the street to retrieve a ball without looking. If it wasn't for my mother, who caught the motion of my skirt dancing away in the corner of her eye and who'd chased after me, I may have been hit by the black SUV that was headed my way.

When my mom and I made it back to the sidewalk, she swatted me across the face. "You must *never* do that again," she scolded, before pulling me into a trembling hug. My mother cared deeply, and she was only trying to protect me.

That was the type of fear that Anna was sharing with me, and I immediately understood there was danger. Going back was a big no-no.

My thoughts ceased, and I suddenly felt a pang of guilt rise inside of me.

"You *cannot* go back," Anna warned.

"But…" I tried reasoning with her for a moment. I couldn't. I didn't know how. There was something in that fiery concern that immobilized me and made me feel that arguing was pointless. There was real danger in going back, it seemed.

Honestly curious, I calmly asked, "Why not?"

Seeing that I'd pacified a bit, Anna let go of her tension and began to explain. "First of all, I never got your name."

"Liz," I finally shared with her.

"Liz," she continued in a calmer manner but with a hint of strictness to the emotion. "Seeing as you don't remember anything, I'm going to try to explain this the best I can."

She seemed to struggle for a moment, trying to find a place to start, not really knowing how to put it. "This… afterlife, as you might call it, is… I suppose the best way to put it is the real world."

The real world? I thought to myself, although I still didn't know how to hide much from her.

"I mean…" She seemed to sigh, still struggling. "I'm sorry, it's just hard to explain. You see, when you… are born, it's not an actual physical body as you would perceive it while you're on Earth. What I mean is there's no real physical anything in the… universe, I suppose is the best thing to call it. We're just… this is hard. I haven't had to explain in so long."

She sent out a plea for help, and Eric came to her rescue. He seemed to make more sense. "The best way to put it is that when you're on Earth, or really anywhere you go, you're in a dream. It's the closest analogy I can give you."

Anna took that and ran with it, continuing on her own with the explanation. "Yes, a dream is a great way to put it. But you're not alone in your dream. We all share the same dream."

I was still listening, but I was incredibly confused.

Anna continued. "All we are is just… emotion. We're each a separate entity, just like when you're dreaming, but there isn't any sense of physical form or anything here. That's something we created for ourselves."

This wasn't making any sense to me, and Anna knew that. She paused for a moment. "Perhaps you'd like to take a while to digest all this," she offered.

"Can I ask a few questions first?" I requested.

"Of course," Anna replied.

"Why is it so dangerous that I go back?"

"We created these dreams to feel more, to experience more emotion," she explained. "That's what it's all about. If you go back, especially when you don't understand things right now, you could compromise the sense of reality of the dream for others."

Now I had even more questions. I couldn't pinpoint which one I wanted to ask first. "If all we are is emotion, why do we need to dream to feel it?"

"Because we need something to stimulate our emotions," Anna told me. "There's no war here. There's nothing to fight over. There's no conflict—apart from your situation. I haven't felt this much emotional stimulation since my last life."

"Your last life?" I asked. "Like reincarnation?"

She thought about this question for a moment. "In a sense, I suppose."

Eric was sitting on the sidelines, still listening in, but he took this opportunity to jump in and give an explanation. "Each time you die in the dream, you wake up. If you want, you can always return to the dream, but you don't get to be yourself anymore. That body's gone—that part of the dream is done. You get to be someone else."

I tried to absorb all of this information, but it was starting to become too overwhelming. I went back to one of the questions I previously had. "So, nothing's physical? But it feels so real."

"Of course we made it that way," Eric said. "If it

didn't feel real, the events that elicit an emotional response wouldn't have such an impact."

That started making a bit more sense.

"So, let me get this right." I wanted to confirm everything I'd just heard. "This is our true form. Earth isn't a real place. We live for our emotions."

"Pretty much," Eric confirmed. "But just because Earth isn't technically physical in the way we define it when you're dreaming doesn't mean that it isn't a real place. It's as real as you want it to be. Everything that happens—every thought, every emotion, every memory—it really happens to you. It is real."

"Okay..." I tried taking in this information, but everything was still muddled into a confusing mess in my mind. "And I'm supposed to remember how this all works?"

"Yes. Just like waking up from a dream." Anna answered this time.

"So why don't I remember?"

"Sometimes people can get so emotionally attached to a dream that they're not quite ready for it to be over," Anna told me. "When they wake up, they're so focused on the last life they lived that they can't see past it."

I sat there in silence for a moment, trying to make sure I had it all down, but I still couldn't organize it all. "How many lives have I lived?"

"We don't really keep track," Anna admitted. "Time doesn't apply here like it does on Earth. That's a concept that we created for ourselves. We've been here forever and dreaming just as long, and we'll keep dreaming forever."

"But Earth has only been around for so long, and people have only recently evolved," I pondered. "It's such a short amount of time when you compare it to forever."

I felt a shift in Eric's emotions, and it seemed like he was laughing at me, teasing me for still being stuck with my Earth-like notions. "Earth isn't the only place where people dream, Liz," he informed me.

"Oh."

"There have been innumerable dream settings, and there will be countless more to come," he explained. "In fact, there are incalculable dreams occurring at this moment in different settings. Different planets, different universes, different idea sets all together. And the people who aren't dreaming are here. Some are simply enjoying the bliss, conversing among each other about their last life. Others are simply taking a break from the difficult emotions that they recently endured."

That struck me as odd. "So how many people are there?"

"Immeasurable," Eric answered.

Wow. This was mind-blowing.

"Where are they all?" I asked the question, even though I wasn't sure I would understand the answer.

"All around us," Anna shared.

It was difficult to catch on at first. I was still left wondering despite her answer. *Around us.* I searched a bit deeper, past my own emotions and those that Anna and Eric were sharing with me, and I suddenly realized there were other emotions flying everywhere. They weren't being pushed upon me or shared with me, but there was a trace of individuality with each emotion. It was difficult to pinpoint which emotions people were sharing with others.

As I reached into the crowd, it almost felt like eaves-dropping. It was like we were all in a giant room and people were having their own conversations, yet I was too involved in my own that I didn't realize there were other people there at all. But the crowd was too confusing, and each emotion overlapped one another like voices at a party.

I quietly paid attention to the vast range of conversations and emotions all around me, and I was struck with awe, trying to calculate exactly how many people were here and how big the room would have to be to house them all.

"You're still stuck on the laws of the Earth," Anna informed me, and I was pulled back to our conversation, yet now that I was aware of the others, I could sense their emotions in the background. "You can't think so three-dimensionally. It's not like that here."

I continued wondering, my mind racing. "So where do those laws and ideas come from, then?"

"From us." Anna put it so simply.

"From us? You mean, like, we come up with the laws of physics together."

"Pretty much," Anna answered.

"If there are so many people out there and so many dreams occurring, how do you two know so much about Earth?"

"Because we just came from there," Eric informed me. "We're headed back, too."

Sensing a hint of confusion in me, Anna continued elaborating. "When one dream starts, most people stick with it until it's over. Once it's over, you move onto a new one. Some people jump into dreams that are already occurring, and others break off and create their own together."

"Once it's over?" I asked. "You mean, once the world ends?"

"Well... yeah. It has to end someday."

"Why?" I continued the questions, utterly confused at how this "universe" worked. At the same time, I was honestly intrigued, although the thought of getting back to Adam was my main priority. If I knew what was going on, maybe I wouldn't have to be without him. "I mean, if you can create the laws and everything, why can't you keep the dream from ending?"

Once again, I felt a glimmer of laughter come from Eric. "We can't control everything. We set the laws down, outline the rules of the dream, create the setting, and then we live in it. We don't write the story before it happens. We let the events run their course. What would a world built for emotion be like if there was no surprise to it?"

I pondered what he said for a moment. "But what about fate?" I challenged. "What about when two people meet and they swear they've met before, and they're sure that some outside force brought them together?"

"That's usually a mutual agreement between the two parties," Eric explained. "But you can't make life-altering fateful decisions for the entire population of the dream."

"You're saying that love at first sight is real because people have met here before?"

"Sure. A lot of the time," Eric answered. "Sometimes they meet here, or sometimes it's in a previous life—the same dream but in a different body. They might fall in love in those bodies and then promise to find each other in their next life."

So Adam and I really had met in a previous life. *But... how?* I wondered.

Eric answered, although my question was directed at my last thoughts, not his. "It's all about emotion. If you create an emotional connection in one life, it will linger onto the next. You'll be drawn to whatever emotionally speaks to you. In this case, it's another person. There are many different ways to love a person—you could be parent and child in one life, and siblings in another, or lovers in another. Sometimes you're drawn to a place, and sometimes it's a simple hobby."

This was so much to take in. I simply sat there for a few moments, not pressing any thoughts upon the others, but trying to sort through all the confusion.

"Can I be left alone with my thoughts?" I asked. "I need to sort through all of this."

"Sure," they replied.

And just like that, they were gone, leaving me alone. I didn't feel completely abandoned, though. They were still nearby, but I knew my thoughts were private now.

I attempted to clear my mind, to wipe away all worry, fear, and inquisition that was rising inside of me. It was difficult. I was stressed and confused, and I just wanted to get back to Adam.

I couldn't rid the questions that were dancing through my head. Some of them were the simplest things that I shouldn't have been worrying about. How do you dream within a dream? Others were more in-depth and serious. How did we feel emotion here in the white mist if we didn't have brains to convey them? How long do people wait between lives before they choose to go back into the dream?

I let these thoughts dance around in my head for what seemed like an eternity. What did I know? Maybe I *was* thinking for eternity. When I had no more questions to ask myself, and when I was content with the way I'd sorted out my racing thoughts, I put my mind back to Adam. I looked back upon my memories once more, and I tried reaching out to him again, just to know he was okay.

I realized there was danger in going back, but it was painful sitting here alone with my feelings without being in the comfort of Adam's presence. What would I tell him if I went back again? What if he saw me?

I knew the others were keeping an eye on my emotions, because I could feel them nearby. If I tried calling out, they would instantly send their warnings again like a slap across the face.

I didn't know what to do. I wanted to curl up in a little ball and cry. Or die, but I already did that.

I think I would rather wish for nonexistence than this nonsensical place. How long would I have to be here alone with my thoughts until Adam came to greet me?

Thoughts and memories continued to come and go. If there was a sense of time here, I would have guessed I was sorting through my thoughts for days. By now, I was a bit more calmed down, as if I'd been in a little ball crying my eyes out and there were no more tears to cry.

I stayed in my bubble, reaching back into my memories, quietly calling out to Adam, praying I could go back and check on him one more time and maybe even talk to him.

I continued thinking, and then I thought some more, my mind finally learning to grasp the concept.

After I had contemplated my confusion for what seemed like a very long time, I settled into my happiest memories from my life, trying to hold on to what I had left. They weren't all just memories of Adam. I looked back on my mom, too. I remembered my dad. I recalled the incredible moments that we would have together before my mom died. Those moments didn't mean anything at the time, but they meant the world once they were gone. It was the little things—dinners, movie nights, and walks in the park. I turned back to it all, reliving my life once again.

Then I hit the moment I met Adam, and I relieved our life until the moment of the crash. As I re-experienced how the headlights spun over the road and the car crashed into the tree, I felt someone calling out to me.

Was my time up? Did I have enough alone time? I didn't feel like I had. And it didn't feel like either Anna or Eric was beckoning for me. It felt like the last two times I went back, only this time, it wasn't just Adam's voice I heard. I heard a large crowd of people calling my name. I *heard* it.

"Elizabeth Marie Janssen," they all called out to me at once, each voice familiar, although I couldn't place them when they overlapped like that. They were summoning me home, back to Earth. I could feel it, and I wanted to head toward the sound of my name.

Without trying to give anything away, I took a giant leap and sprung toward the sound of the crowd. As I did so, I became aware of the caution pulling me back. Anna and Eric were keeping an eye on my mood, but I grabbed on to the beckoning too quickly, and I slipped away under their careful watch.

I found myself able to see the world once more, to really use eyes that I didn't physically have. When I got my hearing back, I heard sobs coming from every direction. People were sniffling, and a man was wailing loudly. A young woman spoke over the sobs.

I regained my sight. I was in a large room with a high ceiling. The room had white ornate walls with a decorative wooden border at waist height. A large window sat to my right, and it let the sunlight shine in off the fresh snowfall.

Surrounding me sat a large crowd of people filling the room, most of them dressed in black. There was an aisle running up the middle of the room, and I was standing directly in the middle of it.

I looked to the front of the room, where a podium was situated off to the right, but that wasn't the center piece. In the front of the room stood a dark mahogany casket, closed and covered in a flower wreath. Next to the casket on an easel sat a large photo of my face.

I recognized the picture. It was cropped from the photos Adam and I took to announce our engagement just months earlier. In the photo, I wore a grin that announced I was the luckiest girl in the world.

I took a few steps back, really trying to take in and understand the scene. When I reached the back of the room, everything became crystal clear.

I was at my own funeral.

CHAPTER 9

My eyes roamed over the room, still in complete shock of what I was experiencing. I was at my own funeral. And there were people mourning for me. When I realized all these people were here for me, *large crowd* became a bit of an understatement.

Why were people mourning for me? I didn't have any friends. I hardly had any family. I didn't expect so many people to care enough to say their goodbyes to me, especially over a closed casket that was full of nothing but my crushed, purple-speckled body. What were all these people doing here?

I always thought that by the time my funeral rolled around, my family would all be gone and that if he was still alive, Adam would be the only one there to say his good-byes.

Then it suddenly occurred to me. This couldn't be real. Not this many people cared about me. I was surely dreaming.

It was absurd. I wasn't dreaming, and I knew that full well. I could feel how real this was, even if I didn't want to accept it.

I scanned the scene a second time, really trying to take it in and to understand who would actually take the time out of their day to shed a tear over me.

My eyes first landed upon the man in the front row who was howling. His shoulders shook, and his head hung low. I watched as his hand came up to wipe his tears every now and then. There was a woman beside him with long, red flowing hair that looped around in tightly woven curls. She had her elbow rested on the back of his seat and was gently stroking the man's back to comfort him.

It only took me a second of watching the couple until I realized the man was my father and the woman sitting next to him was Janelle.

I continued taking it all in, and my eyes shifted to the podium at the front of the room. There was a young woman behind it speaking into a microphone that the room probably didn't need, although it helped the audience better understand what she was saying between her sobs.

The girl had two colors in her hair, and I could see a sleeve of tattoos sticking out from under the three-quarter length sleeve of her dress. It was Shae.

Behind her stood another man, who was quite a bit taller than her with an athletic build. He was letting her speak as he gently stroked her shoulder, trying to calm her sobs. *Cody.*

"Liz was one of my best friends," Shae said as she wiped her nose with a tissue. "We were completely different people, but I admired her spirit. I'm just… crushed that she's gone."

Shae's tears sprang to life, and she turned from the microphone into Cody's arms. She was finished with her speech.

How late had I come in? I wondered.

Cody led her from the podium back down to her seat.

I watched as the most beautiful man in the crowd stood from the front row and made his way to the lectern. Even with yellow fading bruises, he still looked beautiful.

Adam stood at the front and looked out upon the crowd, but he didn't show any indication of seeing me like he had before.

"I'd like to invite Liz's father, Jeff, to say a few words

if he'd like," Adam said softly, gesturing to my father in the front.

My father's wails quieted as he nodded his head. Adam took his seat as my father walked shakily up to the front, followed in toe by Janelle.

He closed his eyes and took a deep breath before beginning. "Liz—Liz was my only child, my pride and joy. She was everything to me. Liz was always so caring of other people, so full of empathy."

He took a moment to gather his thoughts and continued. "When Liz was nine years old, her mother got sick with cancer. Her mother's condition continued to worsen even though they had her on treatments."

Oh, Dad, I thought, trying to send out my love to him and comfort him a bit. I could see the pain happening all over again. The pain he had to live through once with my mother's passing was coming back and tearing him apart.

His sobs didn't cease, but he continued his story anyway. "One night, after Linda was released from treatment—after she had lost all her hair—she was lying in bed, fighting her illness and completely exhausted. This wasn't long before her death, and she was weak. Liz decided to do something about that."

With tears still gleaming in his eyes, he looked up with a smile as he recounted the memory. "Liz went into the bathroom, found a disposable razor, and ran it across her scalp."

He made the motions, as if he had an invisible razor in his hand. "Once freshly shaven, Liz went into her mother's bedroom, lay beside her, and they went to sleep together."

He began sobbing louder. "They never knew it, but I got home from work and peeked in on them. I saw the most beautiful two women, both hairless, lying beside one another."

If I had my physical body, I would be fighting the lump inside my chest, trying to force my heart back down my throat. I would be rebelling against the tears, and my heart would be thrashing, reliving this emotional memory.

"That's the kind of empathy Liz shows, and it's—it's a shame that the world has lost that." My father broke out in wails once again, and Janelle led him back to his seat.

Adam stood up once again. "I'd now like to open the floor to anyone else who would like to say a word or two about Elizabeth." As he went back to his seat, several people simultaneously stood.

I was awestruck at the many people who wanted to say something about me. Did I really make that much of an impact? I never quite believed that.

Adam's mother was the first one to the lectern. As

she began to speak, I was completely overcome in shock to the fact that these people thought so highly of me. Were these honest words, or were people just trying to bring out the best in me?

His mother spoke about how sad she was that I would never become her daughter-in-law. She went on to say other nice things about me, but I was too busy scanning the crowd, overcome by curiosity to see what kinds of people were filling the room.

Much of the room was full of Adam's family members. Most of them lived in the area, but were still visiting for Christmas. How long had it been? Just a few days, I guessed, although my perception of time had been altered while I was in the bright mist.

I stopped listening to the words coming from the speakers, and they simply became muffled sounds that I couldn't process. I was too busy scanning the audience, and I was completely overwhelmed with emotion, each face taking me back to a different memory.

I walked up the aisle backward, exploring faces starting in the back. One of the first faces I noticed looked familiar, but I couldn't place the guy. Somewhere inside that manly unfamiliarity sat familiar boyish features. Was that…? It *was*.

My first and only boyfriend before Adam was sitting in the back row at *my* funeral. I'm not sure if I would call him a boyfriend. Logan was more of a good friend who shared my love of books and went on a few dates in high school. But I had lived halfway across the country then. And he came *here* to tell me goodbye? I hadn't seen Logan in years.

He never stepped up to say anything. Or had he already said something before I came? I didn't think so. But he was here nonetheless, still caring about me after so many years.

My eyes continued up and down the rows. People from school who I hadn't talked to in years, coworkers who I barely even knew, patients who I had nursed back to health. They were all there.

Did I really make an impact on *that* many people? I must have.

After my eyes crossed past each face in the audience, recognizing most of them and passing the strangers off as the guests' family members, I realized that several people had already spoken and sat down. Janelle had said something, although I never heard what it was. One of Adam's brothers had spoken, and now one of my good coworkers, Liana, was speaking. Two of my previous patients were wiping their eyes and preparing their own good-byes.

I was still completely awestruck, and I didn't think this feeling would go away any time soon, but it didn't take long before people stopped approaching the podium. My attention turned from the audience back to the lectern.

Adam was back at the microphone. "If everyone who wants to say something has had the chance, I'd like to close with a few words of my own before we adjourn."

I knew that if I had a heart, it would be pounding out of my chest right now. I had the urge to cry, although I didn't have the ability. I was so overwhelmed and touched by everything that was happening. My attention focused solely on Adam's features and his words as the rest of the scene seemed to disappear around him.

"Liz was—oh, what can I say about Liz?" His question was rhetorical, stalling his struggling words.

"She was everything." His voice was soft, full of grief and longing. "I mean it honestly when I say that I've never met anyone like her. She had a sweet side, but there was a wild side about her that she'd never let you see. It's something that… that really made her unique."

He cleared his throat. "One of the things I've always loved about Liz is how strong and independent she was. She always had her nose in a book, and it gave me time to really study her. It's given me so much time to really understand her. And you know what? She had the heart of an angel."

If my tears worked, they would be flooding the room

by now. I felt touched by what he was saying, knowing that he honestly believed these things and felt that way about me. I felt hurt because I could never touch his beautiful face again. I felt a sense of appreciation knowing that all these people were here because of me. And then I felt every emotion in the room pouring out upon me, and I was soaking it in. All the mourning going on was pushed directly onto me, and I was mourning for myself.

"You know what she told me once?" Adam looked down at his hands, reaching back into his memory and avoiding the eye contact of the crowd. "She told me she became a nurse so that she could save people, because no one could save her mother. She said she wanted to really make a difference in people's lives and that if she could just save one life, she could relieve the pain and suffering of an entire family. If there was one thing I could wish for, I would wish that we could bring that type of spirit back into the world, that Liz could come back and bring her magnificent heart with her."

This seemed to strike a nerve, and he began sobbing uncontrollably. His father moved to the front and finished with a few closing remarks, and soon, people started shuffling, grabbing their belongings.

I stood in the middle of the aisle, still unmoving as people stirred about me. As Adam stood, his eyes made a gentle sweep across the room. I was staring directly at him, and his eyes were full of tears. As his eyes moved past me, he didn't show any indication of my presence until a split second later, after his eyes had moved past where I was standing. In a flash, his eyes jerked back in my direction, doing a double take.

His eyes searched for me, but there were people shuffling around the room now that even if I was standing there in physical form, he would have had trouble finding me.

His double take told me he saw me for an instant, and I wanted to get to him and let him know I was there. I was too overcome with a mix of emotions that I wasn't thinking straight. The idea that I was at my own funeral and was *dead* didn't even occur to me. All I knew was that I hadn't been with Adam for days and that I missed him with every fiber of my being.

I floated through the crowd, passing through their bodies. When I reached Adam, he had shaken off the idea of my presence and was no longer searching for me. Instead, he was making conversation with the guests who passed, shaking hands and thanking them for coming as they headed toward the door.

I stood in front of him, simply staring. *See me*, I begged silently, but he merely continued shaking hands.

When the line slowed and the room emptied a bit,

Adam crossed his hands in a gentleman's stance and gazed around the room at the remaining guests, preparing to shake hands as people left.

I stared up at him, completely amazed with the façade he was putting on even though I knew it was killing him inside. His eyes gleamed with the tears he was holding back.

Knowing he couldn't hear me, I began to speak. "Thank you for your words."

He didn't look down at me or appear as if he knew I was there. Forgetting what I was doing, I reached my hand out to him in habit and placed it on the side of his shoulder.

"I love you," I told him, and just like that, his eyes jerked down at me, gaping and completely full of shock.

He saw me. *Again.*

I felt a sense of giddiness rise inside of me, and I knew he was looking into my eyes. He was frozen in astonishment, yet his gaze gave him away.

He was, by some miracle, able to find his voice. "Liz."

Before he could say anything else, a man stepped in front of him. I couldn't see who it was because the man walked directly where I was standing.

"I'm sorry for your loss," the man said quietly, and I could tell he was shaking Adam's hand.

"Thank you," Adam acknowledged graciously with his gentleman's tone of voice.

The man must've distracted him, because when he moved toward the door and left me in Adam's direct sight, Adam could no longer see me, staring past me as if I wasn't there.

I wanted to speak to him, to touch him again and tell him that I loved him, but before I could, the room began fading. Washing away in a slow, smooth manner, the room, the small talk, and Adam's exquisite face vanished. I wasn't jerked out of the real world like before, but I knew what was happening.

I was going back into the bright mist.

CHAPTER 10

Anna and Eric seemed angry at me, but they didn't push these emotions on me like they had before. Feeling their parent-like disappointed stares, a wave of guilt passed over me.

"I'm sorry," I apologized, only partially honest. I didn't feel bad about seeing Adam, but I knew I'd done something wrong. "I know I'm not supposed to go back."

"You *can* go back," Eric answered matter-of-factly.

"Then why are you so mad?"

"Because you can't go back like *that*."

"Then how *do* I go back?" I was willing to accept that there were rules I may not understand, but wanting desperately to return, I would do just about anything.

Anna answered. "You have to go back to the dream with a fresh start." Realizing that I didn't completely understand her answer, she elaborated. "As a new person. With a new body. As a baby."

A baby? If I went back as a child, Adam and I would be twenty-three years apart. The life we'd planned to live together would never be possible. Adam would have to move on, and I would have to start over.

My heart, already broken and torn, seemed to shatter into a million more pieces. I could go back, but I could never go back to Adam. We could never go back to the way things were.

I quickly became overwhelmed with these ideas, and if my body was working, that knot inside my chest might have suffocated me by now and my tears may have drowned me.

Despite my pain, I wanted more questions answered. I wanted to really understand this place. If I understood it, maybe I could learn how to get back to Adam, and even if it took eternity, we could be together again.

"How long does it take to get back?" I started my series of inquiries.

Eric took the turn of the teacher. "However long you want."

"Well, how long have you two been here? When did you die?"

They both seemed a bit taken aback by the personal

question, but they weren't so shocked as to reluctantly answer my question.

Eric answered first. "I died in 1999."

Eric understood the horror that rose within me. As he said this, I wondered if I would also have to wait decades to return.

"Liz," he attempted to calm my fright. "I'm choosing to stay. I'm waiting for someone."

That made me ease up a bit, although it struck me how long he's been waiting. I became increasingly curious about the life he lived. "How old were you when you died?"

I could tell my questions were beginning to become a bit too personal, but Eric seemed willing to answer. "I was thirty-six when I died."

"How?" My thought was quiet, almost a rhetorical question and only fed by my curiosity, but Eric answered anyway.

"I owned a garage, and one of the cars I was working on fell off the platform and crushed me. It was a freak accident."

"Who are you waiting for?"

"My wife." The thought was simple, and it held a bit of pain behind it with a small hint of longing. "She was pregnant when I died. I'm waiting to greet her."

That thought passed by me almost unnoticed, but in

a double-take, I quickly caught it again. "Greet her," I thought. "So people really do greet their loved ones in the afterlife."

"Yes," Eric confirmed.

"What about you, Anna?" I wondered. "How long have you been here?"

Anna seemed a bit more unwilling to answer, and I got the sense that she didn't want to because she was afraid it would hurt my feelings or scare me.

"The 1800s," she finally answered. Before I could formulate any opinion about the answer, she quickly continued her explanation. "Don't let that discourage you, Liz. I had a hard life, and I've been relaxing here. You can go back anytime. You could go back immediately if you wanted."

I did want to go back, but I was suddenly even more intrigued.

"What happened to you?" I could feel her pain as the question took her back through her memories, and as soon as I asked it, I regretted it. The question clearly hit a nerve. I backed away. "I'm sorry. You don't have to answer that."

"No, I want to." Anna took a moment, as if she was taking in a deep breath and calming the nerve I had just nearly severed. "I want you to understand why I haven't gone back for so long."

One more moment of relaxation and she went into her explanation. "When I was a young teen, a neighbor boy took advantage of me. I don't want to frighten you with the details, but it didn't happen just one time. I was constantly abused, physically by this boy, and emotionally by my father. It didn't end there. When I became of age, my parents forced me to marry a man I didn't love. In fact, I despised him. I spent the rest of my life in a miserable home, struggling to take care of my children, children I had with a man I never loved."

The short snippets of memories she shared with me, the ones that translated into these words, held little meaning compared to the level of sorrow, regret, and torture that her memories brought back. The amount of abuse she endured throughout her entire life was unbearable to watch.

I suddenly felt a pang of guilt rise inside of me, and my heart fell. Was it fair that I was trying so desperately to get back to Adam and to my happy world when there were people suffering like this? Was it fair that I never suffered like that and that I should be given happiness for no apparent reason?

"That's why I haven't gone back yet," Anna told me. "I just need a long break from those emotions to make up for the pain and suffering I endured for years."

My thoughts went quiet now, full of remorse for this

woman. "Why do we have those emotions, then, if they're so hard to deal with?"

"Because we all have a choice," Anna said. "Some people choose to make bad decisions that affect others, and others make good choices. What matters is what *you* choose and how you respond to it. I went into the world on a flip of a coin, and I ended up in a bad situation. I'm not responsible for how those people treated me, but I can choose to heal from it—and I can do that *here*. I'm just taking a break. I'll return to Earth when I'm ready."

"You said you went into the world on the flip of a coin. Is it not always random?" I wondered.

"No," Anna explained. "You always have a choice before you enter the world. You can choose to enter the world blindly—as I did in my previous life—or you can go wherever you want. Most people choose to go where they're most emotionally attached already. Some people might feel emotionally attached to a culture, so they'll return there. Others feel emotionally attached to a family, and they'll come back as their own grandchildren."

My thoughts shifted toward Adam's family. I remembered meeting his niece Lila, and Adam had once told me that his sister named her after his grandmother. He'd said that the ironic thing is that she reminds everyone of their grandmother.

Could it be? I wondered to myself.

"What about names?" I asked. "Why do you two have names here? Were they the same names you had on Earth? What about if someone goes back? Do they have the same name?"

"You can choose your own name, so if you want people to call you something else here than they call you on Earth, you simply choose what you want," Eric said. "Most people like a uniform name, so they'll stick with the same one throughout their lives and while here."

"But your parents name you on Earth," I pointed out. "How can you choose your own name?"

"It's all emotional," Eric said. "Parents can feel their child's name because the soul communicates with them, although they can get it wrong sometimes."

For a moment, only one of his words stuck. *Soul.* I liked the sound of that.

"Adam has a niece who's named after his grandma. Are they the same soul?" I asked.

"Very possible," Eric answered.

I mulled this over in my head, glad I understood one more thing about this world. "Eric, what happened to you when you came here? Did you remember?"

"Yes. I've heard of people forgetting, but I've never actually run across it. You're the first I've seen."

"And what about you, Anna?"

"I remembered, and it was a relief, but I've seen two other people forget."

"Why did they forget?" My thought was again small, somewhat scared how their situation related to mine.

"One of them had just finished waiting decades to reunite with her lover. They returned to Earth together, but she died during the birthing process. It took a long time to bring her back because she had the mind of a newborn. She had been so prepared that she already established an emotional connection, but her preparation betrayed her."

"What about the other one?"

"She actually reminds me a lot of you, and it wasn't that long ago. The woman had died of cancer. She'd been suffering for years and was ready to move on, but her husband wasn't ready to let her go. Because of his emotional attachment, she wasn't able to remove herself from her past life. He was keeping her there, and she didn't remember anything for nearly three years."

The situation sounded familiar, and my anxiety sprang to life as I considered the possibility. No. Not possible.

Nervously, I asked a question I knew I might regret. "What was her name?"

"Linda."

No. This wasn't possible.

"Did she have a daughter?"

"If I remember right, she had a daughter named Elizabeth."

Oh. My. God. My mother.

"Is she still here?" I demanded. They hadn't caught my last thought, and they didn't know where my question was leading. I wanted to feel my mother's embrace and cry into her shoulder, even if she didn't have a physical shoulder for me to cry into.

"I think so." Anna gave the thought with a hint of confusion, curious as to what my stern feelings really meant. "Why?"

Before I could give her an answer, I felt her emotions shift from curiosity to realization. "Oh. You're Elizabeth."

Eric's emotions mirrored the shock of Anna's, and suddenly, Eric's were all I could feel, as if Anna had left our group conversation and was making her way through the crowd. I reached my thoughts into the vast range of souls and went searching for Anna, trying to figure out where she went. Eric trailed after me.

My thoughts floated past other conversations, but there were so many souls conversing, I couldn't pinpoint where Anna was. I wanted her to tell me more, but with so many emotions running wild in this place, I couldn't find her.

I felt like I was racing through a tight group of people in a ballroom. Each were indulging in their own conversations, while some were sitting on their own and experiencing private emotions, but it simply seemed like noise that I couldn't focus on or make sense of.

I felt lost for a moment, and as I slowed down my search and felt like sinking to the ground, my face in my hands, and crying, Anna returned.

"Liz!" She greeted me with excitement. "Liz, she's still here!"

Suddenly every tangled emotion I felt that told me to wail vanished. I could still feel Eric beside me, and by some force that I couldn't understand, I knew Anna had not returned alone.

Another woman came with Anna, and I knew without anyone telling me that it was my mother.

CHAPTER 11

Her emotions swirled around me, and I was quickly soothed by the feeling of an embrace, wrapping all my thoughts and feelings in a comforting hug. All my fear and anxiety melted away.

Anna and Eric slowly slunk away, giving us privacy.

As many emotions that I had felt since the accident—pain, confusion, sorrow, guilt, hope—none could compare to what I was feeling now. I was suddenly overcome with joy being next to my mother after so long. At the same time, a wave of pain swept over me as my thoughts turned back to my memories of her death.

I broke down around her embrace, unable to mask my emotions. I began crying. Hard. Not physical tears, but the feeling of shattering from the inside out was the same.

"Elizabeth." Somewhere within me, I could feel her stroking my hair, although I no longer had any hair and she didn't have hands. "I can't believe it's you."

"Mom." I couldn't hide my astonishment.

Countless questions ran through my head. What happened to her? Why didn't she go back yet? What does she remember?

"Mom, I'm… completely stunned."

"I know, Liz. Anna told me. I'm a bit stunned myself. I didn't think I'd be seeing you so soon. You've grown so much!"

"I have so many questions."

"And I have much to tell you."

"It's all… so confusing."

"Tell me about it." She seemed to roll the eyes that she didn't have, and it soothed my mood.

I'd lived half my life without my mother. I always believed she was gone, and I had settled with the idea that I would never see her again. Being here with her was simply overwhelming. My heart ached for her, wanting to get to know her again and loving her as much as I always did. There'd been so many times throughout my life that I wished she was still there. My father did his best, but he wasn't my mom.

My mom was here now, and I had so much to confide in her that I forgot about everything else.

"I missed you so much," I told her. "Anna said you were like me. She said you didn't remember this world when you died."

"Yes," my mother admitted.

"How did she find you just now with so many souls here?" I wondered.

My mother answered my question calmly, seeming to understand how difficult this was for me. When she shared her emotions with me, things didn't seem as confusing, and it calmed me.

"Here, we recognize people by their—for lack of a better explanation—emotional fingerprint instead of their face. Since there's no space here, Anna simply had to search for that emotional fingerprint and explain the situation so that I could connect with you."

"Can you tell me what happened when you died?" I asked, curious how our situations compared.

"I was sick for a very long time. I was ready to go. I didn't want to leave, but I knew it was inevitable. Your father didn't want me to go. It tore him apart."

I was suddenly jolted back to my memories of my father. After my mom passed, he went into a deep depression for nearly three years.

When I was young, dad used to take me to the zoo with him so I could visit the animals. After my mother's passing, he didn't take me to the zoo until I was fifteen.

Instead, he'd spend most of his time in bed. Sometimes, I'd crawl into bed next to him, and we would just talk.

My father still cared about me. I knew that, but I could also see the pain on his face. It took him a long time to recover. His recovery wasn't an immediate change, but slowly, he got back to his feet, although I knew he'd never gotten over her.

"I remember," I said.

"He spent years holding on to me. For most of the time, I thought I had some unfinished business that needed taking care of, but I couldn't figure it out. I knew you were safe in your father's hands, and I didn't have anything left but the two of you."

"Did you ever visit him?" I asked.

"No. I was prepared, and I also believed in an afterlife. I knew I was dead, and I didn't feel like I needed to go back."

Our situations were very different, I realized.

My mother continued with her story. "For a long time, I was stuck in a state of confusion. Other souls explained it all to me, but I still couldn't remember anything. I was scared. Your father clung to this idea that I was coming back. He thought that was the way he was supposed to feel and that there was no other option. After three years of this, your father eventually decided he needed to be taking care of you, not hurting himself over something he couldn't control. Once he stopped holding on to me so tight, everything became clear. I could remember again."

I thought about this for a moment, comparing it to Adam. Was that what Adam thought? Was that why I couldn't remember? Or was I the one thinking those things?

"Tell me about him," my mother said.

"Dad's a lot better now. He has a girlfriend, and she's super nice."

"I wasn't talking about your father. I was asking about the man who holds your heart."

Adam? How did she know?

"He's magnificent," I told her, and then like two teenagers, we began chatting about boys. I had never talked to my mother about boys, and it was such a relief to have her here now.

I jumped far into the details, telling her all about Adam. I started from the beginning and replayed all my memories for her as if we were watching them on a television screen. She asked questions as I went along, but mostly she was enjoying everything about me that she missed.

"Oh, Liz." Her thought had a sense of excitement to it, knowing that I met a wonderful man and lived a happy life the way she wished. The other part of it held a hint of apology to it. Was she apologizing because she wasn't there? It wasn't her fault.

Reading her thoughts further, I understood where the apology came from. Through all the good I'd shown her, hints of sadness had slipped through. I hadn't intended for her to see that. I choked back the stifling memories and shied away from her. I didn't want her to see me hurting.

"It's okay," she encouraged. Soft, caring emotions enveloped me. "I'm here for you. You don't have to hide from it anymore."

I didn't realize until that moment how long I'd waited to hear her say that. When her soul brushed up against mine, my spirit seemed to fracture at the edges. Something broke within me. All the grief and sadness I'd held back for so long rushed to the surface. I couldn't stop the memories from flooding out of me as I shared the weight of every crushing memory with her.

I sat at my mother's bedside in the hospital room, choking back sobs. I didn't want to be too loud and wake her—and I knew once I started crying, I'd never stop.

Dad had gone down the hall to get us food. He had a habit of forgetting to eat these days, and more often than not, I wasn't hungry anyway. My stomach twisted as I took in my mother's frail form. She was hooked up to all these tubes, and she'd lost so much weight. Mom didn't want me to see her like this, but I knew why Dad had brought me to visit.

My pulse pounded in my ears. I had to do something to distract myself. I stood and went over to the window, where a bouquet of roses withered on the sill. I ran my fingers over the dying petals, and tears welled in my eyes. Dad and I had brought the flowers last week. It was absurd how quickly time could change things.

When Mom first received her cancer diagnosis, her window was full of flowers. It was like a garden. Dad had made it my job to water the flowers, and I had fun tending to them while Mom read me stories from an old children's anthology.

Then she started treatment, and she was getting better... until she wasn't.

We'd been given so much hope, only to be crushed under the weight of her diagnosis all over again. Nobody had sent flowers this time. We were all so used to her being in and out of the hospital that we could hardly remember a time when she wasn't attending doctors' appointments or chemotherapy sessions.

But this time was different. Dad wouldn't say it out loud, but I overheard the doctors say they expected her organs to fail any day now. I didn't want to believe I'd heard them correctly. I couldn't imagine a world without my mother in it.

"Hold on just a little longer," I whispered to the roses. I was delirious to think they'd listen.

My mother cleared her throat, and I whirled around to see her eyes fluttering open. I quickly rushed to her side and took her hand.

Her gaze roamed over me, like she was trying to memorize my face—though it looked like it took every effort to do so. "Liz, you're here."

"I'm here," I told her. "Dad's just down the hall."

Mom winced. "You should be in school."

She was trying to make a joke, but it fell flat.

I crinkled my nose. "I like it better here. My teacher doesn't tell stories the way you do."

Her lips turned up at the corners ever so slightly. "If you came for stories..."

Mom tried to lift her hand to point, but she could barely do it. I followed her gaze, and my eyes landed on the anthology next to her bed.

"How about I read one this time?" I suggested.

Mom relaxed deeper into the bed, while I grabbed the book and sat beside her. I began reading out loud. I couldn't read as fast as she could, and I stumbled over some of the words, but Mom helped me when I got stuck.

I finished the story, then turned to set the book aside. I caught sight of Dad in the doorway. He'd been watching.

Tears beaded at the corners of his eyes, but he wore a smile, like he'd never seen anything more beautiful in his life.

"Is anyone up for a picnic?" Dad asked.

Mom couldn't go anywhere, so we spread our food out across her bed and laughed while we ate. Dad told stories of him and Mom from before I was born, and Mom smiled the whole time.

By the time the nurses kicked us out of the hospital room, I could swear the roses on the sill stood straighter than before.

We got the call early the next morning.

Dad held me while we sobbed, and my grandmother came over to watch me while Dad left for the hospital. I couldn't remember much of anything that happened until the funeral, nor could I recall the months that followed.

When the pain started in my abdomen, I thought it was a product of grief. Nothing had hurt this much since I'd lost my mother, and I figured it was my body's way of communicating the agony.

Then it got worse. It felt like knives had been stabbed through my lower gut. I worried it was cancer.

Dad took me to the doctor, but nothing came up on the imaging tests. I hated being back here. The smell of latex gloves and lemon floor cleaner reminded me far too much of visiting my mother when she was sick. I feared my fate may end the same as hers.

The pain worsened, until it became debilitating.

The doctors suspected appendicitis but couldn't find any sign of infection. After six months of ruling out every possibility, they scheduled me for laparoscopic surgery and found the endometriosis. The doctors promised the condition could be managed, but it meant future hospital visits and multiple surgeries.

Dad was so distraught that he punched the doctor in the face. Luckily, the doctor didn't press charges.

I sobbed for over an hour as I clutched the painful stitches on my abdomen and heaved into a bag the nurses had provided, but nothing came up.

Years passed. Some days I couldn't tell if the pain in my abdomen was real, or if it was only my grief. I dove into stories to distract me from it all.

Then came the doctor's visit that I'd never forget. I could still hear the doctor's words echoing in my mind. "The tests show you aren't ovulating. I'm sorry, but the results indicate you may never be able to have kids."

I wasn't sure I'd heard him right. I was still young—too young to even be thinking about kids right now. But I always knew I wanted them some day. I was certain there had to be a treatment for this.

There wasn't.

My body was going to do whatever it wanted, and if that meant it broke me... then so be it.

Sorrow racked my soul as I relived the harrowing

memories I'd tried so desperately to ignore. These were the most emotional, vulnerable parts of my life. My mother's passing was the most painful, and it was difficult helping my father through his depression. Then when I got sick, it was physically daunting and emotionally stressful. Living with the fact that I could never have kids struck a nerve every day. Every time I saw a woman with a newborn, it felt like a knife through my heart knowing I would never experience that. Reliving it all again made it all too real.

My mother's love surrounded me from every angle, permeating my soul from the inside out. I could feel how much she cared.

And yet inside, I was breaking. "I admired you so much," I admitted. "I wanted to be like you. Then I got my diagnosis, and you weren't there. Why couldn't I have kids? If the world is all part of a dream, why couldn't I choose? That just doesn't seem fair."

"Just because we are creators of our world doesn't mean we can control everything that happens," she reassured me. "Sometimes we make things happen, and other times it's unpredictable. It's what we do with those unpredictable scenarios that define us."

I had the thought that the unexpected was painful. I was apparently thinking my thoughts aloud, because my mother responded.

"Yes, some of the strongest emotions come from the unexpected, but think about all the unexpected moments in your life that have given you pleasure, happiness, thrills, enjoyment, and comfort."

I took myself back through my most vivid memories. I reminisced about the pond, my twenty-first birthday, and Adam's proposal. But I didn't just look at those memories.

I replayed my graduation ceremony and recalled how ecstatic I was at the time. I remembered the first time I rode a rollercoaster, and I recalled the adrenaline that thrilled me. I thought back to the time Shae and I had a sleepover and watched chick flicks all night, throwing popcorn at the screen when the guys acted like jerks. I looked back to the first time I gave CPR and saved a patient's life in the hospital. I took myself back through it all, everything good that ever happened to me.

My confidence grew as I reminisced.

And then I thought of what else I did. When I wasn't going to school, comforting my father, or holding Adam's hand, I was usually reading a book, and it suddenly occurred to me why I was such a bookworm.

Each character I read about conveyed their emotions onto me. When they fell in love, so did I. When they were angry, I felt angry, too. When they cried, I cried. I'd used stories to feel something… yet all this time I'd been avoiding my own story.

Something struck me that I'd never been brave enough to admit to myself before. "All this time I thought not being able to have children was some sort of character flaw, like I wasn't a whole person without that experience. But I was wrong. I am whole and complete, and I have been all this time."

"Yes, you have. Difficult times will change us, but they don't have to wreck us," my mother said. "Nobody chose for me to have cancer, but we chose to be there for each other through it. We can take these hard times and use them to deepen our understanding of ourselves and others—to make connections. Do you understand the purpose now?"

"I'm starting to," I admitted. "There are moments I can't control or predict, but I have the power to face them and find meaning in whatever way I choose. Our experience in this life is about the choices we make. We have the choice to work to make these bad things not happen, and I'm a part of that because we're all connected. Good things don't always have to come out of the experience for it to be valid, but maybe that's not the point. It's not all about feeling the good and shunning the bad. They're all part of the same experience."

Comfort washed over me, and it was in that moment

that something within me shifted. The heavy weight lifted from my heart. For the first time, my soul felt light.

"I know you're desperate to remember," my mother said compassionately.

"Yes. I really *do* want to remember, but I'm afraid to let go. Do you think I'll be with Adam again?"

"You can go back, but things won't be the way they were before. It's time to start anew."

"How do I do that?" I wondered. "How do I… let go?"

"It's not about letting go, but *allowing* yourself to process it. The grief will always be a part of you, but there's so much more to you than that."

I pondered this, until I realized something. "If we're all connected, then maybe I can't do this on my own."

A moment of clarity struck, and I understood everything I needed to do. My mother released me from her embrace, and I slowly retreated.

"I'll be back," I told her.

"I'll be here waiting," she replied.

I called out Adam's name. It was difficult this time, but after a few moments, I could hear him calling out to me, too. I held on to the sound of his voice, and I found my way to our bedroom with ease.

Adam was sprawled across our bed, his hair in a mess and bags under his eyes. It didn't look like he'd slept well in weeks, and his bruises were nearly gone. Had I really been gone that long?

"Liz!" He was shouting in his sleep, and his body convulsed. In an instant, he was calm again, his eyes still closed and his face now relaxed. "Please don't die," he whispered.

I took my spot in the bed next to him and reached my hand over to his. "I'm here," I said with a soft voice I could actually hear. I placed my hand on his, and I felt his kind, beautiful energy pour into me. "I love you."

His eyes shot open, and he jerked away from me. He tumbled off the other side of the bed. A heavy *thud* sounded, and a beat passed before he peeked over the edge of the mattress.

His voice came in a breathless whisper. "Liz?"

CHAPTER 12

His fear didn't last long. Adam poked his head back up over the bed, taking a long look at me. He wore a puzzled expression.

"It can't be you," he whispered. He inched toward me.

"Please don't freak out," I begged.

"I'm not freaking out," he assured me. Perhaps it was the sound of my voice, but his fear seemed to fade away now. He crawled back onto the bed next to me.

We sat cross legged on the bed facing each other.

"How?" Adam couldn't seem to formulate a sentence, and his eyes widened in astonishment.

I had a difficult time finding my words as I stared into his blue eyes. My eyes traced every aspect of his face, moving down to his lips, then back up to his nose, and finally to his eyes again. It was like I was trying to memorize every inch of him.

"Are you an angel?" he asked.

"Why? Am I radiating?" I joked, which made him smile.

"Liz, you've always radiated." He paused for a moment. "Am I dreaming?"

I thought about his question for a moment. "I don't know."

Had I entered his dream? Was that possible? I looked around. It seemed real enough to me.

"No," I told him. "I'm pretty sure this is real."

"Then how are you here?" His voice broke for a second, and I knew my presence was hurting him. He thought he'd lost me, and now I was back.

I wanted to tell him that I loved him and simply enjoy small talk with him. I wanted to ask him how his day was and cuddle up to him, but I knew my time was limited. At any moment, I could be jolted back to the afterlife without warning.

I gathered what strength I had, but it was extremely difficult to reveal my purpose without shattering his heart. I took a moment to calm myself.

"I'm here to convince you to let go," I told him gently.

Tears began falling from his eyes now, slowly and without a sound. "Let go?" He looked at me longingly and shook his head slightly. "Liz, I can't. I'll never forget you."

His hands reached out to mine, and although I couldn't feel him, I could sense a change in my emotional state. I could feel him in my heart. Not my real heart—the one that pumps the blood I no longer had—but in the heart that housed all my emotions. He shivered.

"You don't have to forget me," I promised. "Take everything we've ever done—everything we've *felt* together—and let it inspire you. I know you'll do good in the world, Adam. I'm just glad I got to be a part of that."

His eyes fell shut, and I instructed him to sleep. His body fell to the pillow, and I soothed him as he fell back asleep, whispering to him and promising the same thing he promised me not too long ago.

"We'll see each other again," I vowed.

He opened his eyes one last time and looked at me. "Don't make promises you can't keep," he whispered.

"I promise," I repeated. As if my promise magically soothed him, his eyes closed, and his breathing slowed.

Once he was asleep, I pulled back to my mother, and I found myself once again in the bright mist.

"Are you okay?" she asked.

"I will be," I told her confidently. I didn't know what

the future had in store, but I knew we could choose to make it better.

My mother embraced me again, and I completely relaxed. I didn't know how long we sat there exchanging stories, but I knew I was laughing and crying and feeling free.

One moment I was conversing with my mother, asking her questions about the universe and talking about her past lives, and the next, my questions ceased. There was no reason to continue asking them because I had all the answers myself. At the snap of a finger, all this knowledge instantly flooded me, and everything I was confused about suddenly became crystal clear.

I knew how the universe worked. I knew all about my past lives. I suddenly understood the concept of no space, no time, and no physical form.

Adam and I really *had* met in a past life. Several, actually, and we were about to meet again. Countless memories came at me, and I could see the lives I'd lived. There were just a few on Earth, but my lives stretched far back to infinity into other dreams. Some places were similar to Earth while others were completely different universes.

I said farewell to my mother and waved her goodbye, but before I was ready to return, I sent her one more question. "Why haven't you gone back?"

"I wanted to make sure you made it home safe."

My heart warmed. I turned from her, and I let all my recently acquired knowledge disappear. I jumped back into the dream world, but this time, I wasn't stuck in a state of limbo. When I arrived, I was in full physical form.

EPILOGUE
ADAM

After Liz died, people kept telling me things got better with time. I wasn't sure I believed them. Time had caused this in the first place. For so long, I had wished time would've stopped that morning, that we'd never gotten out of bed and I could just lay beside her for eternity.

But time kept moving forward, no matter how much I wanted to stop it. I had to take life hour by hour, until those hours became days, and those days turned into weeks. An all-consuming darkness enveloped me.

I'd dreamt of Liz after the funeral, and she'd promised me we'd see each other again. I looked for her everywhere. I saw her face in so many crowds, and heard her voice in so many places—but it was never her.

Five years passed, and I clutched a copy of her book at my side. It was a children's anthology, and I knew it'd meant a lot to her. When I'd given her things back to her dad, he insisted I keep this. I'd read it so many times that the cover had become tattered and worn.

The sun warmed my skin and glistened off the trees in the park as I approached an empty bench. My dog wagged her tail and panted happily when I sat.

"Which story do you want today?" I asked her, flipping through the pages. She loved sitting at my feet and listening to the stories.

She barked, and I noticed something had caught her eye across the park. I followed her gaze to see a group of kids around a picnic table. Art supplies scattered the table, and a little girl with pigtails wiped paint across her friends' nose. The kids' laughter rang across the grass.

One of the adults called the kids over to another table for food, but the little girl hung back to finish her painting.

My dog barked again. Before I could tell her to stop, she took off running. Her leash flew out behind her as she sprinted across the park.

"Elizabeth!" I called, but it was too late. She didn't hear me, and instead skidded right up to the girl with the pigtails and licked her painting.

I ran as fast as I could to catch up with her. "I'm so sorry," I apologized as I grabbed Elizabeth's collar.

The girl couldn't be more than five years old, and I worried she'd start crying because her painting was ruined. Instead, she started to laugh. "I love puppies!"

She reached out to let Elizabeth sniff her. My gaze traveled down to the table. The girl had been painting a rock, but Elizabeth had turned her artwork into a blob. It looked like she'd been painting a slug, but only the head remained.

"I'm sorry about your painting," I said.

"That's okay," the girl giggled. "Things get hurt some-times, but with a little bit of care, they can become something new."

She dipped her brush into a glob of purple paint, then made a swirl around the slug's body. "Now it's a snail!"

I stared down at the painting, her voice echoing in my mind. She spoke so innocently, like her words applied only to this painting, but I knew they meant so much more.

"What's your dog's name?" she asked.

I tore my gaze from the painting. "This is Elizabeth."

"Hey, that's my name!" she stated proudly, pointing to herself.

"Liz!" a woman called.

Something in my chest twinged at the name, but it quickly settled.

The woman approached us. "I'm so sorry. She loves dogs. She has to pet every one she sees."

"Can I get one, *please*?" Liz begged.

Her mother laughed. "We can talk about it when we get home. Right now, it's time to eat."

"All right, I'm coming," Liz grumbled, before turning back to me. "It was nice meeting your dog. You can have this."

Liz stretched her hands out, and I instinctively reached out to take whatever she held. She dropped it into my hands, then skipped away to get some food. I looked down to see it was the rock she'd painted.

I showed Elizabeth. "Perfect for my collection."

Elizabeth barked happily in agreement.

"Come on, girl." I grabbed her leash and led her back toward our bench. I shot one last glance behind myself at the little girl.

Time hadn't fixed me, but maybe that wasn't the point. I used to think losing Liz had broken me, but perhaps like this rock, it wasn't about becoming the man I was before—but becoming something new. I'd become a new man after I met Liz, and I'd changed after I lost her, too.

Perhaps that change didn't need to destroy me.

For the first time in five years, I felt something stir in my heart—a beacon of hope. I'd spent so long enveloped by darkness I thought would never end. But the darkness couldn't last forever. Where there was light, there could be no darkness.

And so, if you kept walking, sooner or later you'd find where the darkness ends.

About the Author

Alicia Rades is a USA Today bestselling author of young adult and new adult paranormal fiction. When she's not dreaming up magical stories, she's either binge-watching Netflix, meditating, or spending time with her family. She has an unhealthy obsession with psychic characters and writes with a deck of tarot cards next to her computer. *Where the Darkness Ends* was her first published title.